SHADOW ON THE MOON

By
JOE GIBSON

I0541431

ARMCHAIR FICTION & MUSIC
PO Box 4369, Medford, Oregon 97504

*The original text of this novel was first
published by Ziff-Davis Publishing*

Armchair Edition, Copyright 2010 by Gregory J. Luce
All Rights Reserved

IMAGINE GANGSTERS IN ROCKET SHIPS!

Man had reached the moon. And now, with scientific technology striding quickly forward, the possibility of consumer rocket ships was at man's fingertips. However, the Earth's most vile dictators and criminals sought to steal top scientific secrets that could threaten the skies and perhaps even the spaceways themselves, casting an ominous shadow on the moon.

It was up to a tough World Police Inspector to see that this didn't happen—and when the crisis landed in his lap, he soon found he had far more to worry about than the contemplation of his gorgeous secretary's beautiful legs.

FOR A SECOND COMPLETE NOVEL, TURN TO PAGE 87

CAST OF CHARACTERS

TOM ROURKE
On the surface he was just a public relations manager for a big aeronautics company, but what was his secret purpose?

RALPH McWILLIAMS
The owner of AiRockets incorporated. All he wanted to do was put a rocket ship in every American's garage.

MANNY BORSACH
He had a tough job—to keep rocket ship technology from falling into the hands of a powerful criminal organization.

ROBERTA SIMAKOV
She was dedicated to her father—a brilliant scientist. But her attention was soon stolen by a daring undercover agent.

SKID HALLOWAY
If you needed someone to test fly a new experimental rocket ship, Skid was your man.

CZECMELOWEICZ
He approached AiRockets, Inc. with a proposed profit-sharing deal, but he had a lot more in mind than big business.

MISS FINCH
She was Rourke's beautiful secretary. Fortunately for Rourke, she gave a low whistle every time he walked by.

CHAPTER ONE
To the Home of the Scientist

"NEW YORK is on the line, sir." Rourke's secretary sent her voice through the intercom in dulcet-toned warbles.

Tom Rourke stopped pounding the typewriter to whirl around in his swivel chair and reach across his desk, flipping a switch from *intercom* to *videophone.* The wide, twenty-four-inch screen exploded its frosty white expanse into a sharp color image.

"Hi, Tom." Bill Warner's fleshy features were creased in a smile. The advertising manager of *Spaceways* magazine wore a snappy blue suit with a scarlet silk kerchief tucked in at the throat. On the wall behind him was a blowup of a *Spaceways* cover, featuring the S-90, the Earth-Moon supply ship. "I got this advertising layout on the AiRocket experimental ship here on my desk," Warner said. "That what you're calling about?"

"Right," Tom affirmed. "Can you have one of your staff artists delete the control surface from that rudder? Research just told me we're using a solid rudder fin—no break between rudder stab and movable control surface."

Warner, who wasn't an aeronautical engineer, frowned in puzzlement. "Rudder stab and control surface?"

"That line showing a break in the rudder surface," Tom explained patiently. "Delete it. It'll be a solid rudder."

"Oh..." Comprehension dawned on Warner's cherubic face.

"We want the ad picture to be as up-to-date as possible," Tom said. "After the experimental job's tested, there'll probably be a few more changes; the final production model will be slightly different. But we don't want it too different; we want the people to see pictures of this experimental job and get used to the ships before we put them on the market."

"Okay." Warner nodded. "I'll take care of it for you. Say, how about an article on the test flight?"

"For *your* magazine?" Rourke taunted jovially. "Are you sure airockets would fit in with galactic space—tales and time-travel adventures?"

"It's science fiction, chum," Warner retorted. "But the boss man has already asked about such an article. After all, you guys are the first ones to give Mr. Average Man his own little rocket ship."

"Uh-huh. Pretty good angle." Rourke grabbed a pencil and scribbled a notation on his desk pad. "But I'd prefer to wait and see how the test flights turn out. It could be a flop, y'know. How long before I'd have to give a definite answer?"

"I'll ask. Maybe we can leave a hole for you and plug it up with a short story if you can't come through. Thirty-five-hundred words okay?"

"That's a big enough hole."

"I'll let you know." Warner grinned and waved a pink hand. The screen went frosty blank.

Rourke flipped it off and started to turn back to his typewriter, but the little signal-light winked blue again. He flipped it on. The screen blinked into color and the gray-haired visage of Ralph Henderson McWilliams, President of AiRockets, Inc., glowered from it.

"Tom, my boy, stop chasing that secretary and toddle up here to Daddy's office," he commanded in stern mockery. "The devil just walked through the Main Gate. I want you to be present when I spit in his eye..."

"Okay, Mac." Rourke switched off and climbed onto his feet.

MISS DOROTHEA FINCH gave a low, caressing whistle as Rourke breezed through the outer office. He raised a hand in fond farewell, feeling that nice glow in his tummy that Miss Finch's whistles always gave him. Miss Finch was, after all, a very neatly stacked blonde, even if it was a false blonde. She had nice, tanned legs below her short, flared whipskirt, and a very firm bosom supporting her plunging neckline. It was something to be considered whistle-bait by a gal like that. He proceeded down the long, wide corridor to the elevators, a crooked grin lingering on his face. He had a strong, appealing face, as the girls around Administration had duly noted: a firm jaw, strong mouth, cool gray eyes beneath dark brows, and curly dark hair. Mr. Thomas Rourke, twenty-seven, Advertising & Public Relations Manager for AiRockets, Inc., and a bachelor.

He took an elevator up to the fifth floor and strolled along another corridor toward McWilliams' office. The outer wall of the corridor was transparent, looking out over the wide company airfield. There were the big hangars looming in squat rows along the edge of the field, and the curved, sprawling plant buildings behind them. A small personnel jetcopter stood out on the parking ramp, but the rest of the field was empty, the big hangar doors closed and lifeless.

It wouldn't be lifeless a few months from now. AiRockets was a new company, pioneering a new type of aircraft. The complete layout represented a good half-million dollars. When experiments were concluded and production began, the airfield would be humming with activity.

Rourke entered McWilliams' outer office, waved dutifully to the battery of secretaries, and strode casually through the entrance labeled PRIVATE in big chrome letters.

MAC WAS sprawled wearily behind his nine-foot curve of desk, a stubby cigar protruding from his granite jaw. He waved a blunt hand to the big chair beside the desk. "Better strap yourself in for some high maneuvers," he said.

"Bullock just called from the Main Gate, saying a Mr. Johann Czecmeloweicz"—he pronounced it "Smellowitz" and paused, then, to spell it— "Of Volks-Aero Industries, Limited, has arrived from Budapest, Hungary, to have a little chat with us."

Rourke slid into his chair, hiding the sudden excitement within him under a completely blank expression. "What's Volks-Aero Industries?" he asked in feigned innocence.

Mac stared at him, exasperated. Then he explained with mocking patience, "Volks-Aero just happen to be the leading jetcopter outfit in Europe. They've had the European and Middle East jetcopter markets tied up for years, freezing out all American jetcopter interests—"

"And our little rocket crafts are due to upset their apple cart," Rourke concluded swiftly.

Mac nodded. "Sometimes you almost sound human. This Czecmeloweicz is an agent from Aero Solicitors of Budapest, he says they're legal representatives for Volks-Aero. So check your guns; he should be in here any minute."

Rourke settled himself comfortably and lit a cigarette. He was accustomed to Mac's verbal references to aerial warfare; the Old Man had been a teenage jet fighter pilot when the UN was playing checkers with the Chinese Reds, using Korea for a checkerboard—which had been all of fifty years ago. Mac was a sly old-timer in his late sixties, as tough as tempered steel, with a right leg from the knee down of plastic, sponge rubber, and aluminum tubing. He'd been around.

Mr. Johann Czecmeloweicz entered with the pompous air of a man accustomed to liveried servants and cocktails at four. He was a plump, middle-aged man wearing dark suit, cravat, and bowstring tie in the Continental fashion. Introductions were politely exchanged and he seated himself before Mac's desk, balancing a thick black briefcase precisely upon his knees. He spoke English with a clipped accent.

"Now, gentlemen, to business," he said. "As you know, I am here as legal representative for Volks-Aero Industries, Limited. My clients are exceedingly interested in your…ah…novel enterprise, here."

"I can imagine," Mac drawled wryly. "You will find, Mr. Czecmeloweicz, that we have registered our Statement of Intent with the UN World Commerce Commission, to license our airockets legally to local manufacturers in both Europe and the Middle East for the usual royalties."

"But you have not yet filed an International Patent on your rocket craft, Mr. McWilliams."

Mac shook his head. "We aren't out of the experimental stage, just yet. But our Statement of Intent covers the patent application."

"Yes, of course. Providing your rocket craft works."

Mac stiffened. "Just what do you mean by that?"

CZECMELOWEICZ gave him a bland smile. "It is understandable that my clients express doubt as to your success, Mr. McWilliams. Jetcopters have been manufactured for the past thirty years as an accepted, trustworthy product. It has provided the safest private transportation in history, and its affect on your American society has already been profound. All you Americans live in country homes, your major cities becoming mere commercial centers, your small towns virtually disappearing into thin air. Jetcopters are a worldwide success. However, your *rocket* ships…" He shrugged complacently.

"The jetcopter replaced the automobile easily enough," Mac growled irascibly. "But you didn't come here to argue about that."

"Indeed not," Czecmeloweicz agreed. "My clients may express doubt in your enterprise, but they also believe in caution. Should your craft be successful, naturally they would become a dangerous competitor to Volks-Aero jetcopters. We are willing to compromise by purchasing a controlling interest in your company's stock."

"A contro—" Mac broke off, choking on the words, and stared unbelievingly at the calm, self-assured little man. Slowly, Mac parted his thin lips and got his wind back. He kept his voice as flat and smooth as the surface of a frozen lake. "Naturally," he said, "you expect to be thrown out of my office."

"I merely hoped you would consider the matter," Czecmeloweicz corrected him, completely unperturbed. "I shall be here for one week. You may contact me at the Hotel Atometro."

"And if I don't?" Mac spat at him.

Czecmeloweicz repeated the delicate shrug of his shoulders. "I shall return to Budapest and inform my clients that you are not interested, naturally. But I hope you will reconsider." He rose, smiling. "For your benefit, Mr. McWilliams, I shall wait one week."

Then he gave a curt bow and strode to the door. It closed firmly behind him as he went out.

Mac stared after him through a long moment of silence. Then the Old Man slouched back in his chair and swiveled to face Rourke. "What d'you make of that, sonny boy?"

"I make a dog-eat-dog fight of it," Rourke answered quietly, leaning forward to flick his cigarette ash into the tray on the desk. "Volks-Aero will probably drag us into World Court on charges of Capital Exploitation, if we don't cut them the big slice of our cake."

Mac snorted derisively. "Volks-Aero wouldn't have a legal leg to stand on. People accepted the jetcopter over the automobile because most of the world's highways—particularly our own—had practically crumbled to pieces, what with government funds going to defense and traffic overload pounding the roads to bits. Governments latched stiff highway taxes on the people, and the people retaliated by buying jetcopters. Now everybody flies."

"But they do indeed fly jetcopters," Rourke remarked comprehendingly.

Mac gave an emphatic nod. "They've accepted the windmills. Jetcopters are easy to fly and they're safe. Anything breaks on her and she automatically sets her rotors to let you down slower than a parachute! The world has accepted them and will continue to do so for some time to come.

"That means they won't accept our airockets so readily. The airocket is new, different. And because of that, Volks-Aero can no more claim Capital Exploitation than the Martians, if there are any. All they can claim is that we'll be breaking their jetcopter monopoly in Europe—and it's about time somebody did. They haven't improved their copters by a single bolt or rivet in the past twenty years!"

"They don't have to," Rourke retorted, grinning. "Nobody else can compete against them so long as they continue to buy the complete commercial franchise in every European country. We're the only ones who could compete, since our private airockets come under a separate franchise."

"AND THEY can't buy up those franchises unless they manufacture airockets themselves," Mac muttered worriedly. "So what the devil did this character expect to gain by coming here? A 'controlling interest' in our stock, huh! What'd he mean by that?"

"Well, they certainly knew we'd turn them down," Rourke concluded. "So now it's their move again. Whatever it is, it'll probably tell us exactly what they do mean."

"Ummm. Smells bad." Mac kicked his chair around and

glowered down at the airfield spread below his window wall. "If I didn't know our atomic rocket unit is the only one of its kind on Earth, I'd think they were going to manufacture airockets and freeze us out."

*You don't know how close that is to the truth...*Rourke thought, staring at the back of the tousled gray head. Aloud, he said, "I guess there's nothing we can do until they've shown their hand. It could be a complete bluff, or they may have expected us to be no more than a shoestring outfit. Maybe they thought we'd jump at the money if they offered to buy stock to—"

He broke off his rambling suppositions and both men turned as the outer door opened.

A middle-aged secretary stood framed in the light. "The tower just reported Skid Halloway coming in, Mr. McWilliams."

"Thank you, Miss DeVries." Mac swung back to face Rourke. "Get down there and meet him, will you, Tom? Tell him I want to see him. He starts test flights on the XR-1 tomorrow morning and this thing today has me worried—"

"Want me to call Bascomb and Aimes?" Rourke asked. The law firm of Bascomb, Bascomb and Aimes handled AiRockets' legal affairs.

Mac shook his head. "I'll call them later. If this guy is going to hang around for a week, there'll be plenty of time to check with Volks-Aero and Aero Solicitors of Budapest to make sure he's *bona fide*. Get Skid Halloway up here."

"AiRocket Tower to N-five-two-eight. Commence final approach at three miles, altitude seven-fifty, compass twenty-nine degrees. Report for clearance, over."

"Five-two-eight to tower. Wilco, over"

The flat, metallic voices came from the little radio speaker behind Rourke's head. He was sprawled in the reclining seat of the three-wheeled field scooter, waiting down on the parking lane for Skid Halloway to come in. He lit a cigarette and gazed into the warm blue afternoon sky, expectantly.

"Five-two-eight to tower. Am in final approach, gear down, props set. Over."

"Five-two-eight, you are cleared for landing. Use Runway Seven: wind south-southeast fifteen miles. All private craft diverted from your approach. Over."

"Roger, all clear."

THE PLANE appeared first as a tiny black splinter near the horizon, then grew rapidly in size. It was an old government surplus UN Patrol Fighter—one of the famous Lockheed PF-170's flown by the old UN Combined Air Fleet when world preparedness had cancelled all possibility of the Soviet Union's ever winning an atomic war; and the world waited for Russian policies to change to more peaceful intentions, which finally happened with a somewhat bloody purge inside the Kremlin. The UN Patrol pilots had cut a dashing figure in world history during their brief, happily inactive careers. Their close-fitting blue uniforms, designed to be worn under the old insulated, air conditioned, pressurized flying suits, had affected men's clothing styles so that snug-fitting suits were now the fashion.

But the old PF-170 was still a good aircraft. Particularly for companies whose business demanded an occasional fast trip of five thousand miles or so. With her big, counter-rotating supersonic props driven by gas turbines, she could cover long distances as fast as a jet plane, burning less fuel than either jets or reciprocating engines. Many companies had hastened to buy the worn, surplus planes, despite the fact that they accommodated only a pilot and one passenger, formerly a radar operator.

Skid Halloway flared his N-528 out and eased her tricycle gear neatly onto the runway. She slid across the field, braking her headlong speed, swung easily into the taxi strip, and came rolling over to the parking lane with her big props fluttering noisily.

Rourke nudged the little field scooter into gear and drove over to meet her.

The props whirled to a halt and the thick, pressurized blister swung back over the cockpit. Halloway waved a greeting and clambered down from the big, fat fuselage with a plastic carton under his arm. Rourke stopped the scooter and waited for him.

"Well, if it isn't old commercialism himself!" Halloway exclaimed, grinning. "How's the advertising business, Tom?"

"Fine," Rourke answered. "How's the flying business?" He felt the usual tingle of awe as he grinned up at Halloway's wide, freckled features. Skid Halloway had been on the third expedition to the Moon, had walked the surface of another world. He was a short, stocky man thirty-four years old; retired, now, since he was too old to stand the physical strain of space flight. They had other young men to take the ships out to Lunar Base now. And the first expedition had landed on Mars.

"Me and the flying business is going to have a cup of coffee," Halloway replied, tossing the plastic carton into the back seat and crawling into the scooter beside Rourke. "Had some nice weather in Pittsburgh. Nice and soupy, with thundershowers."

Rourke swung the scooter around and headed back toward the streamlined pile of the Administration Building. "Mac wants to see you, Skid. He says you start test flights on the XR-1 in the morning."

"What?" Halloway said somewhat indignantly. "What gives with the Old Man? I've just finished a forty-five-hundred-mile jaunt to get a spec analysis on that rocket nozzle for him. Man, if I've got to crawl out at two in the morning to test-hop his pet rocket—"

"I think he wants to speed it up," Rourke cut in pensively. "It looks like somebody may try to give us some trouble."

"Trouble…what kind of trouble?'

"Commercial franchise trouble, maybe." Rourke flicked his cigarette ashes over the side of the scooter. "A legal representative from Volks-Aero Industries, Limited, paid us a cal this afternoon. Mac'll tell you about it."

"Okay, but what's the pitch?" Halloway frowned in puzzlement.

"I don't know for sure," Rourke answered half-truthfully. "Mac can't figure it out, either. But just between you and me, Skid, I'm going to ask you a favor."

"Sure, Tom. Name it."

Rourke turned to look at him, levelly. "When you climb into that XR-l in the morning, *be damned sure it hasn't been tampered with…*"

HALLOWAY accepted the advice with a nod and a thoughtful silence. They pulled up before the building steps and left the scooter, entering the wide, cool corridors within. Rourke clapped Halloway's shoulder, said he'd see him around, and went back to his office. Miss Dorothea Finch smiled at him in the wall mirror in the midst of applying her lipstick.

Rourke glanced at the wall clock and hid a grin. It was twenty minutes yet until quitting time. He went on into his private office and slumped into the chair behind his desk. He had twenty minutes to wait. Twenty minutes until all the office people would be gone and the videophone operator would leave the company switchboard on automatics.

He slid down in his chair and swung his feet up on the corner of his desk, then pulled open a bottom drawer and slipped out a heavy clothbound book. The gilt-letter title was

WORLD CRIME SYNDICATES. He flipped it open, extracted a bookmarker, and commenced reading.

...Thus, there is conclusive evidence that the very success of the UNO as a world government, and the mere existence of the UN World Police, is a direct cause of the international criminal organizations and syndicates that exist today.

If there were no UNO, no World Police, the present organizers of world crime would be cozily situated in various national governments as dictators, as military commanders, or as members of political state police. They would go about their chosen profession of brutality, power through fear, and sadistic terror without the slightest thought of possible reprisal.

With the establishment of world justice, enforced by the UN World Court and the World Police, these former despots have been forced underground. They are now struggling for dominance in a new realm: the realm of international smuggling, narcotics, thievery and murder. Recent history has provided them with sound training for such criminal activities. They have developed cunning, resourcefulness, and organizational ability; they are rapidly organizing world crime into a group of syndicates with such far-reaching influence that they may become as great a threat to world security as any powerful nation bent on conquest...

Rourke read on through the pages, smiling grimly. Minutes ticked away in silence. When he finally looked up, it was five minutes past quitting time. He stowed the book back in the bottom drawer, rose and crossed to the door. Poking his head into the outer office he saw that Miss Finch had departed for home. Grinning his satisfaction, he closed the door and went back to his desk, sitting down and flipping on the videophone set.

He dialed a number and waited, lighting a cigarette.

A COLD, thin-lipped face splashed onto the screen.

Beneath the face, a glowing legend ran: United Air Delivery Service—Anywhere in Atom Town. Anytime.

"What can I do for you?" Thin-lips asked. He wore a soiled green undershirt and needed a shave.

"Get me Shadow One," Rourke said. "This is Shadow Nine."

Thin-lips vanished instantly. A tough, square-jawed man with short-cropped brown hair replaced him. "Oh, it's you, Rourke. Anything new?"

"It's here, Manny," Rourke told him.

Inspector Emanuel Borsach narrowed his eyes comprehendingly. "Who is it?"

"Calls himself Johann Czecmeloweicz," Rourke answered, then spelled it. Manny's gaze dropped below the screen's level as he jotted it down. "He said he was from Aero Solicitors of Budapest, Hungary," Rourke added. "They're supposed to be the legal representatives for Volks-Aero Industries, Limited."

"I'll get it off to headquarters," Manny said. "Maybe World Police Frankfurt offices can check it on their files."

"Get it soon as possible," Rourke pleaded. "It maybe urgent. Old Man McWilliams wants to start test flights on his experimental ship in the morning."

"I'll call you back in a few hours," Manny promised. "Your home number?"

"I'll be there. I'm going over to check on Doc Simakov at Southwest Atomics—"

"Don't tip your hand!"

"I won't." A tight grin twisted Rourke's mouth. "But there are two men technically responsible for the airocket. One's old Prof Thornton Weigand, who developed the atomic rocket unit. They won't know about him yet— McWilliams has him hidden inside the company's research labs—"

"And this Simakov? He's at Southwest Atomics?"

Rourke nodded. "The project actually began with his synthetically produced inertium gas. He's written several papers on it for scientific journals, and it's pretty well known that he's tied in with AiRockets, Incorporated. They just might strike at him first."

"Better get acquainted with him then," Manny approved. "Can you approach him without exposing yourself?"

"McWilliams told me he can almost believe Volks-Aero is prepared to go into airocket production as our competitors," Rourke said. "I can take it from there and ask Simakov if he's received any inquiries from Volks-Aero on his inertium gas. That'll give me an excuse to tell him all about this Czecmeloweicz."

"Where's Czecmeloweicz now?"

"Said he was staying at the Hotel Atometro."

Manny grinned without mirth. "We'll put a tail on him. Might lead to something."

"Don't let it lead to his discovery that you're following him, that's all," Rourke warned. "So long as they don't know we're wise to them, they won't be looking for me."

"Right," Manny agreed. "And walk soft on the eggshells yourself, Rourke. If they ever do have reason to suspect you, they'll kill you without hesitation. Good hunting, fellow!" The screen went blank.

Rourke stared at it for a moment, then sighed and snapped the set off. He closed up his typewriter, locked the desk, and rose. Leaving his office, he proceeded along the silent, empty corridor to the elevators. A crooked smile tugged at one corner of his mouth.

Business was beginning to pick up...

THE DECISION had been reached three years ago, in the spacious, glass-walled office high up from the street level in the United Nations Center. A wizened, bald-headed little man known to every intelligence agency in the world had sat behind those soundproof portals labeled *World Police Headquarters* and put his finger on the map where Atom Town, Nevada, was located. AiRockets, Inc. had just been formed—its location was Atom Town.

The decision had been that AiRockets, Inc., was too ripe a plum for a certain world crime syndicate to overlook. This particular syndicate happened to deal in technical and industrial secrets, stealing them and selling them to the highest bidder.

AiRockets, Inc. was a pioneer company founded on a new technical development. It was all too ripe for the picking.

Anticipating the syndicate's interest in AiRockets, the chief had ordered Inspector Thomas Rourke to establish himself in the company and keep his eyes open. So Rourke became an advertising expert. He went to McWilliams with a long dossier of past experience and references in aircraft advertising. McWilliams hired him.

For Rourke it hadn't been an entirely new experience. In the past nine years he had been an Art student in Paris, a graduate petroleum engineer in Arabia, an oil-stove salesman in Mongolia, a musical comedy actor in Russia, and a newspaper reporter in South America. In each case he had received an intensified training to prepare himself for his role.

Now, after two-and-a-half years in which he'd actually prepared a worldwide advertising campaign for AiRockets, his role was finally paying off.

At last the time had arrived for Tom Rourke, Advertising & Public Relations Manager, to take on the added role of Shadow Nine…

He checked out his little jetcopter from the parking lot behind the plant buildings and lifted it into the slanting, golden rays of the sunset. The copter's wheels folded neatly into its hull.

Atom Town spread out in a blanket of low, terraced buildings nestled snugly in landscaped trees, shrubbery and lawns, warm lights glowing from transparent walls to stud the blue shadows of the long, low valley that sheltered them. In the center of the valley, near the silvery ribbon of the river, large plant buildings stood in flat-roofed swirls and curving walls; above them rose the six-mile-high towers of the commercial center, glowing softly in pastel hues against the deepening violet of the evening sky. Tiny motes of light, like blue fireflies, swarmed back and forth over the town in orderly traffic patterns, the jetcopters of the five million residents who lived comfortably within the fifty-mile radius of pleasant countryside.

ROURKE switched on the nightlight in his copter and swung east, past the fringe of the town where he could avoid the traffic patterns. He sprawled relaxed in the reclining seat, his hands resting lightly on the control wheel, gazing out through the transparent, teardrop hull. The turbine hummed faintly behind the seat and the big rotor blades made a deep, soft thrumming sound overhead.

He found a clear patch of sky with no other copters approaching and pulled the wheel back until its column snicked into neutral. The copter eased up as its rotors adjusted, and stood hovering in the faint evening breeze, its nightlight blinking alternate blue and red, warning the other craft of its standstill presence.

Casually, he swung the portable videophone screen across his lap and dialed Dr. Samuel Simakov's home number. The scientist ought to be home from Southwest Atomics by now, but it wouldn't do any harm to make sure.

"What is it please?"

The girl's face on the screen was interesting. Her jet-black hair was curled tightly about her head, twinkling with blue highlights. She had a heart-shaped face with a slender nose, petulant lips and dark, smoldering eyes.

But the interesting factor was the lack of expression, even of curiosity, on her lips—and the deep, haunting look in her eyes. Rourke had seen that look before. It was terror.

"Is Dr. Simakov at home?" he asked calmly.

She hesitated for a moment, then spoke hurriedly. "No, Father won't be home tonight. He has another engagement. Could—do you wish to leave a message?"

"Well, I'm Tom Rourke of AiRockets, Incorporated. Are you his...ah…" Rourke made it sound casual, nonchalant.

"Roberta Simakov. Doctor Simakov is my father."

"Good evening, Miss Simakov. I'm disappointed. I did want to discuss a certain matter with your father this evening. It's rather urgent and, of course, confidential." Rourke smiled cordially. "Could I drop in and discuss it with you? The explanation is involved, I'm afraid, and I wish you'd tell your father as soon as he comes in—"

"I—I'm really—terribly sorry, Mr.—"

"Rourke," Rourke said.

"Mr. Rourke. But I have a date who's waiting; I was just leaving—" The terror had crept into her voice, upsetting its musical timbre. "If you could call Father at his office in—the morning—he's usually there rather early—"

"I'm afraid this is too urgent," Rourke interrupted her. "Can't you tell me where I could find him tonight?"

"I'm—I'm afraid I can't!"

"Then please remain there," Rourke spoke commandingly. "I shall arrive in a few minutes, Miss Simakov. I'm in the air now."

Before she could frame a protest, he snapped off the screen. Folding it back into its niche, he shoved the control wheel forward and sent the copter drumming through the evening sky at top speed.

The Simakov home was over the side of the valley, nestled in the shoulder of a worn sandstone ridge, facing the western sunset over clumps of flowering cactus. It was surrounded by the wild, open Nevada desert country, dotted with the faint lights of other homes nearby. Rourke approached it skimming low over the rolling, boulder-strewn surface. He was seconds away when he saw the blue spark of a jetcopter rise up the face of the ridge and dwindle into the oncoming night sky...

CHAPTER TWO
Killers in the Night

THE TOP speed of Rourke's Oldsmobile jetcopter coupe was one hundred and twenty-five miles per hour at five thousand feet. At higher altitude, where the rotors couldn't bite into the thinner air quite so effectively, the speed was lessened.

He had the rotors set in reverse, braking his forward velocity as he swept over the landing ramp next to the Simakov home. He eased the wheel to neutral as the copter windmilled to a halt, then pressed the wheel down in its spring-mount to descend to the ground. The airspeed indicator registered five M.P.H. against the press of the night breeze, and the radaltimeter clocked the gradual approach of the ground; the synchronizing gears locked and the landing gear unfolded from the hull.

Rourke flipped off the turbine slid the side-panel back, and swung his legs to the ground. Slipping out of the little craft, he strolled with feigned casualness to the small portico entrance of the house. He pressed the door stud and heard the chimes ringing faintly within.

He saw a shapely feminine figure approach through the dark foyer beyond the glass wall; then the door slid back and Roberta Simakov was greeting him in a tense whisper. "Please come in…"

"Thank you for waiting," he said, following her back through the foyer to the soft glow of the living room. The sound of the front door automatically sliding closed behind him sent a nervous tingle up Rourke's spine.

He had a definite idea of what he was going to see. But it wasn't as bad as it might have been. At least there was no corpse on the floor.

Doc Simakov sat on the wide couch before the glowering crystal embers of the electronic fireplace, still very much alive but badly shaken. He sat hunched forward, elbows on knees, with his graying head pillowed in his hands.

An open doorway leading into a brightly-lighted office-den, just off the living room to the right, revealed a scene of vast disarray—books pulled down from shelves and torn papers scattered over the floor. A few minutes more, Rourke thought, staring at it, and they'd have made a bonfire of the place.

"You must excuse Father," Roberta Simakov was saying huskily. "A man just struck him with a pair of brass knuckles—"

Rourke let an expression of profound amazement spread over his face. "What in the world—" he gasped. "What's been going on here?"

"Robbie, call the police," Dr. Simakov spoke through his fingers. Then he raised his head from his hands and managed a wan smile at Rourke. "I must certainly thank you for coming, Mr. Rourke. Your persistence probably saved our lives…"

"Eh?" Rourke grunted incredulously. They had really thrown a scare into the old boy.

Roberta touched his arm. "Do sit down, Mr. Rourke. Please."

"Of course." Rourke moved over to a comfortable chair and slumped into it, facing Dr. Simakov. Roberta smiled reassuringly at her father, then crossed the room to the videophone set in the alcove.

"Now then," Rourke prompted, frowning. "What's all this about, Doctor?"

"I'm not sure I can offer any explanation for it, either to you or the police." Simakov apologized feebly. "There were five men—they wore black masks over their faces! I had just come home and the table was being set for dinner—" He spread his hands in puzzlement. "They forced their way in with guns and held both myself and Robbie here in the living room while they entered my den. They told us to be quiet, to not give them any trouble…that's all they said. Then they went into the den and began tearing through everything as if—as if they thought I had something hidden in there and they were looking for it!"

"Is there something hidden?" Rourke asked. Across the room, Roberta's voice was a soft, insistent murmur as she spoke to the videophone screen.

"Nothing," Simakov answered in deep perplexity. "I—I even asked, what it was they were looking for—I would have given it to them! That's when I was—" He lifted a hand to his cheek.

Rourke noticed, then, the bruise that was swelling and darkening the side of the doctor's face.

"They told me to shut up!" Simakov added grimly.

"ISN'T THERE anything you might have had hidden in your den, Doctor?" Detective Lieutenant Ybarra's voice carried a hard, penetrating tone of inquiry.

Simakov gave him a helpless shrug. "I know of nothing. If there was something valuable I'd have a wall-safe to hold it—but I don't even have a wall-safe."

"What are you working on at the present time? At Southwest Atomics, I mean."

"A new synthetic carbon. It can only be made in small volume, like dust particles." Simakov shook his head. "It has possible uses in the dusting techniques of preparing industrial diamonds, but there is nothing secretive about it. My work is widely published in scientific and industrial journals."

"This synthetic carbon has been publicized?"

"Even the technique of transmuting its molecular

structure has been publicized," the little scientist retorted. "We feel other atomics companies might be interested in doing some research on it."

"And there's no other work you've done that's been kept secret?" Ybarra was a patient man, and thoroughly persistent, for all his lean, wiry physique and emotional Latin temperament.

"Oh, there are a number of things," Simakov replied indifferently. "But they are the well kept industrial secrets of the companies which bought the rights to them. The companies have those—I don't."

"I see." The Lieutenant closed his notebook with a final snap and rose, his dark face grim with discouragement. The two uniformed Sky Troopers noticed it and shuffled their feet impatiently, then leaned back against the wall again.

Ybarra paced over to where Rourke was standing beside Miss Simakov's chair. His dark gaze met Rourke's directly.

"You were coming to see Dr. Simakov on an urgent matter, Mr. Rourke? So urgent it could not wait until morning?"

Rourke nodded. "I called ahead, of course, to see if the Doctor was home—"

"It's very fortunate that you did," Ybarra interrupted with almost a strain of suspicion in his voice, "would you mind telling me the exact nature of that urgent matter?"

Careful, boy...Rourke warned himself mentally. "Why, as I said—it's really a business matter. We have reason to suspect strong competition from a certain European firm, and I wanted to know if that firm had made any inquiries to Dr. Simakov regarding his inertium gas, which is used in our aircraft—airockets, I mean—"

"This inertium gas is an industrial secret owned by your company, AiRockets, Incorporated?" Ybarra prodded him.

"Naturally. We bought the rights to it."

"And if anyone wanted to steal it...they'd find it in your offices." Ybarra nodded solemnly. "Very well, Mr. Rourke. I guess that's all here—" He turned as a uniformed Police Technician came out of the office-den.

"All through in here, Lieutenant," the Technician reported.

"Clear the men out then," Ybarra instructed. "Dr. Simakov would probably like to get his den back in order." He turned and walked back to stand before the little scientist. "We'll do our best on this, sir," he promised, "though I confess there's little to go on. One last question, if you don't mind."

"Of course not," Simakov approved readily.

"Have you received any inquiries about your inertium gas?"

"Why, no—not that I recall." Simakov looked toward Rourke. "What was the name of that firm?"

"Volks-Aero Industries, Limited," Rourke said.

"No, no inquiries from them," Simakov concluded.

"Then that's it. Good evening, Dr. Simakov."

THE SCIENTIST rose and shook hands, then accompanied the Lieutenant to the door. Troopers and Technicians filed out past them.

Rourke gazed after them thoughtfully. He could almost picture the exact images that were flashing through Ybarra's mind: the Lieutenant suspected strongly that either he or Dr. Simakov—or both of them—was lying. Discreet inquiries would be made at both their companies to check their stories.

Rourke wondered vaguely if the crime syndicate had placed any of its agents within the Atom Town Police Department.

They usually did.

"Care for a drink?" Roberta asked.

He became aware of her looking up at him with a quizzical smile. "I could use one," he admitted. "Whiskey."

"Same as mine." She rose and crossed the room to the liquor cabinet, a boyish swagger in her long-limbed stride. "Soda or water?"

"Water." He strolled after her, listening to the dry sounds of voices from the foyer. Dr. Simakov was bidding goodnight to Detective Lieutenant Jose Ybarra.

Roberta finished pouring, turned and handed him his drink, gazing up at him over the rim of her glass with dark, questioning eyes. "You don't like the police, do you?" she asked quietly.

"It's that man, Ybarra," Rourke answered lamely. "A wiry man like him ought to be tempestuous, hot-tempered. He isn't, though—he's a glacier. The man unnerves me…"

Suiting the action to the word he took a healthy swig of his drink. Its warm glow trickled down and burst in his stomach.

"Perhaps that's why he was made a detective," Roberta teased, smiling.

Dr. Simakov came in from the foyer and hurried toward them.

"So Robbie's mixed you a drink? Good!" He reached up and rested a hand on Rourke's shoulder. "Hardly a hospitable welcome for you, Mr. Rourke—police and all that. I'm very sorry."

"On the contrary, Doctor, it was a privilege to arrive in your hour of need," Rourke consoled him with a grin. "Makes the shine on my armor seem a bit brighter."

SIMAKOV broke into an appreciative chuckle. "Well, you certainly came galloping to the rescue!"

"But I didn't even realize it," Rourke protested jovially. "If I had, I'd probably have turned tail and run like a rabbit."

"I doubt that very much, Mr. Rourke." With a bright smile, Miss Simakov moved up close to him, so she was looking up into his face.

Rourke gave her a startled look that wasn't entirely feigned, and shrank away from her. "…Er…Miss Simakov?"

She whirled and burst into a bright, merry laughter that her father shared, gray brows upraised. "Really!" she exclaimed, facing Rourke again. "I think our Prince Charming deserves a kiss…"

"Let's control ourselves, Miss Simakov," he retorted in his best serious tone. That stilled the merriment in her face If she embraced him, Rourke knew she would be thoroughly shocked to feel the holstered guns beneath his padded jacket. He turned his gaze to her father.

"Regarding that matter I came to see you about, Doctor— your company has reserved the rights to your inertium gas for any purposes other than those technically described in the agreement with AiRockets, Incorporated—"

Simakov nodded, busily mixing himself a drink at the liquor cabinet. "The rights are reserved to sell the inertium gas process to other companies for other uses," he affirmed.

"Has any other company bought that process?"

Simakov turned and stared at him with raised brows: "If one has, I haven't heard about it. Be glad to check on it at the company, though, and let you know in the morning." He tasted his drink and came over to Rourke. "Why do you ask? Do you tie it in with this competitor firm—this Volks-Aero Industries you mentioned?"

"There might be a tie in," Rourke said.

"If there was, it would mean some company was using the process for some purpose other than airockets, and then selling it again to this Volks-Aero. Is that what you're driving at?" Simakov peered up at him quizzically. The side of the scientist's face was now stiff, badly discolored. Roberta stared at it with a look of concern.

"It would be decidedly illegal for any company to resell the process to Volks-Aero," Rourke said comprehensively. "We could drag them before the World Court on charges of Capital Exploitation for that."

"Doesn't seem reasonable that they'd try it then, does it?" Simakov asked.

Rourke took another swallow of his drink and spoke over the glass. "Doesn't seem reasonable for a gang of hoodlums to force their way in on you, either."

Simakov's expression went blank. "I still fail to see a connection. What would a raid on my den have to do with reselling the process? I keep no legal documents that would have any bearing on that."

"They may have thought you did," Rourke lied amiably. "Anyway, look it up for me, will you?"

"Very well. I'll call you in the morning."

"Then it's settled." Rourke finished his drink and crossed over to set his empty glass on the liquor cabinet. "I know you two haven't had dinner yet, and neither have I, so I'd best be going—"

"Stay for dinner with us," Miss Simakov suggested quickly.

"I'd like to," Rourke said, grinning—and it was the truth. "But I've another engagement tonight. You'll excuse me?"

She followed him to the front door. Her father shook hands with Rourke, then she followed him outside and took him by the arm. Rourke grinned in the dark, feeling her fingers caress his hard biceps exploringly. She stopped him outside on the portico.

"You will come see us again?"

"Certainly," he promised. "You're quite...beautiful...Miss Simakov."

"For that you can call me Robbie," she exclaimed teasingly. "Good night, Tom—that is your name, isn't it?

Tom?"

"Yeah. Good night, Robbie." He turned and strode briskly out to his copter.

HE HAD a small, seven-room house, set in the trees near the river, on the outskirts of Atom Town not far from AiRockets, Inc.

The living room was a typically cozy sanctum of deep blue and mirror and transparent walls set in swirling lines with curved lumps of furniture clustered about the deep carpet. It had the austere, mechanical perfection of arrangement that proclaimed it a bachelor's abode, unchanged from the precise pattern set by the little multi-armed house robot during the weekly cleaning.

Rourke flipped on the soft glow of the floor lights as he entered. His sweeping scrutiny of the room noted that nothing had been changed, no item disturbed from its accustomed place, nor any footprints in the springy surface of the cunningly telltale rug. Peeling off his jacket, he pulled a Luger from its holster and slipped it into his belt, then threw the jacket over the back of a chair. He crossed the room and sprawled before the television panel facing the full length mirror wall of the screen. The controls rested below his right hand. An auxiliary panel was within reach of his left; he turned to it, pressed a button beneath a small placard of a hot beef sandwich, another under a cup of black coffee. Then content to let the house robot bring it to him, he settled back and flicked on the television screen.

ROURKE found that he was in a spacesuit. He was dimly aware that he was aboard an outbound rocket to the moon. He suddenly remembered that Robbie Simakov was in grave danger. He looked at the disrupter gun in his hand.

Then he heard her scream.

The echoes of the scream weren't too far away. He bounded down a long gray corridor. Dim yellow lights flickered overhead as he ran. There was another scream. It reverberated through an open door leading to the vast inner shaft of the spacecraft.

Rourke stepped carefully through the opening—gun raised. At that moment Robbie Simakov screamed for a third time. Rourke looked up to see her—now strangely with brilliant red hair—climbing up the inner ladder of the shaft.

Immediately below her, grasping at her kicking legs, was an alien being.

The alien was blue-skinned and appeared to be male. He was apparently trying to dislodge Robbie from her hold on the ladder. Rourke looked down and shuddered—the shaft was so deep that the blackness obscured its bottom surface. Without hesitation, he aimed the disrupter gun and fired.

The alien lurched back—and fell.

As the blue-skinned body fell by him, Rourke suddenly heard the musical chimes of his videophone. He opened his eyes to the glare of his television screen.

A GIRL singer was doing a slow wiggle while the chimes of the videophone continued to sound. Rourke shook himself out of the last remnants of his dream and sighed. He flicked the television off and rose. Cramming the last of his unfinished sandwich into his mouth, he crossed the room to the videophone alcove, slid into its seat, and flipped on the screen.

Inspector Emanuel Borsach glared at him. "Stop watching that Channel Thirteen. You're not old enough yet." Then Manny grinned. "We've got a tail on your tail's tail."

"Who?" Rourke asked curtly.

"Police," Manny said. "Followed you from the Simakov home. We caught the alarm on the Police short wave and sent a man out to watch. What happened?"

"Gang of thugs muscled in on Simakov and his daughter," Rourke informed him. "Acted like they were looking for something. I came along in time to break up the party before it got too rough. The local cops are suspicious but you can't blame them—no robbery, no other motive. A Detective Lieutenant Jose Ybarra was there."

"Know him—he's all right," Manny said. "Your pal, Johann Czecmeloweicz, gave the order on that raid, though. We caught him on his way to dinner in the Hotel Atometro. Our boy watched with considerable interest as a waitress gave him a menu—they use girl waitresses there, you know, not robots; high class joint—and this fellow slips an *a la carte* sheet from the menu, slips it into his pocket, then pulls out another sheet and fastens it on the menu. The waitress took his order, carried the menu off, and switched *a la cartes* again when she thought nobody was looking."

"She's their contact?"

"Little gal named Betty Lou Johnson. Lives at the Spaceport Motel, according to Atometro's personnel directory. One of our boys is a bellhop there now."

"Any more on Czecmeloweicz?"

"World Police Frankfurt wants a photostat on him for identification. There is a small outfit called Aero Solicitors in Budapest, and it did handle a small legal matter for Volks-Aero several months ago, but Volks-Aero claims no contract was signed and Aero Solicitors is definitely not their legal representative."

"This is our bunch then, Aero Solicitors must be their front outfit."

"One of them, anyway," Manny agreed. "We'll get a stat of Czecmeloweicz to Frankfurt on the midnight strato-express. Now, brace yourself for the takeoff!"

"Why?"

"Little Betty Lou Johnson got off duty half an hour ago and went down to a bar near the spaceport. She's sitting there now with five tough-looking goons who just landed on the roof in a copter sedan. They've been joined by a chap named Marty Williams—know him?"

"No."

"He's one of the plant guards out at AiRockets Incorporated. He goes on duty out there tonight."

Rourke pursed his lips reflectively.

"And Halloway's supposed to take the XR-1 up in the morning before dawn. Call me if Miss Johnson and her party go out to AiRockets, will you, Manny?"

"I'd thought of it," Manny taunted him. "They'll probably head out there before anyone else is due to show up. Maybe you'd better start on your beauty sleep..."

"Yeah. See you then."

ROURKE buttoned the house robot to dispose of the serving tray and peeled off his clothes as he wandered into the bedroom. He shaved and showered, blew himself dry with unscented air, set the bedside alarm clock, and tumbled into the sheets. His Luger pistol resided cozily beneath his pillow.

The alarm was set for two-thirty. Its luminous hands pointed to 1:45 when he awakened to the persistent, ringing chimes of the videophone. He pulled himself out of bed, Luger in hand, and padded barefoot into the living room.

Manny's rugged features splashed on the screen. "The five goons are sitting in their copter just outside the AiRocket grounds," he reported crisply. "The guard, Marty Williams, just came out to meet them."

"I'm on my way," Rourke yawned, and flicked off the screen.

He returned to the bedroom and dressed carefully. No

padded jacket this time, but a loose, full-sleeved woolen blouse. No shoulder holsters, but a long trench coat with spring clip holsters in the baggy side pockets. He moved like a drab gray shadow through the wet morning fog, melted into his jetcopter, and lifted it on thrumming rotors. The Moon was a cold, bright disc in the black sky, and clumps of trees and buildings protruded blackly from the silvery blanket of ground fog below. He neutralized the controls and settled back, shoving the flop-brimmed gray hat back on his head and lighting a cigarette.

The job before him would probably be the most ticklish task he'd have to perform. The syndicate crooks must be allowed to break into the AiRocket plant and create a disturbance—yet they mustn't be allowed to do any serious damage. They had to be stopped before it became serious—but he couldn't expose himself to them!

There was too much chance that one of them might get away; and if that one should report Rourke as being something more than just an Advertising and Public Relations Manager, the syndicate would quickly make one accurate conclusion: that Rourke was a World Police Inspector. Thereafter, the trap so carefully laid to catch the syndicate would fail—and Rourke's life probably wouldn't be worth a plugged nickel.

So he had to stop them.

HE PLUMPED the copter down on its pudgy tires in the parking lot and used his passkey to enter AiRockets' Administration Building, moving down the dark corridors and up the elevators with the aid of a flashlight. He entered his private office, switched on the lights, and sprawled behind the desk.

The tough, beefy face of Captain Gaines of the plant guards flashed on the videophone screen in answer to

Rourke's call. "Main Gate," Gaines reported gruffly.

"This is Rourke, Advertising and Public Relations—"

"I can see that on the call-board, Mr. Rourke," Gaines reminded him.

"Oh…fine. Are there any rail shipments coming through the Main Gate this morning?"

"No, sir, it's very quiet this morning."

"Well, I'd been wondering if perhaps someone might try to slip through that way. We're testing the XR-1 this morning—"

"Yes, sir, the crew's over at the hangars now." Gaines was respectful, if dubious. "But nobody's tried to slip past here, sir."

Rourke grimaced impatiently. "Well look, Gaines, we've been having some suspicious things happen lately. I wonder if you'd mind checking the guards at their posts?"

"Oh—not at all!" Gaines complied, but his tones were hardly enthusiastic.

"I wouldn't be surprised if there was some trouble this morning, Gaines," Rourke prodded him.

"I'll call the guard posts, sir."

"Fine. Let me know if anything happens. I'll be here in my office."

"Very well, sir. I'll call you if anything happens."

The screen blanked.

Rourke sighed wearily, snapped the videophone off, unlocked his desk, and took the book out of the bottom drawer. Then he settled down to wait…

Notable among the criminal activities of the various world crime syndicates are those activities that grew out of The War Years. The most predominant is smuggling and the black marketing of contraband goods, but this activity is generally conducted by small local groups of criminals very loosely organized into any worldwide order, and as such they are more a concern of local authorities than of the UN World Police.

Next on the list is narcotics, which is the activity of several known syndicates; following that comes slavery, the major activity in the Orient where prostitution is not frowned upon by social custom. One of the most insidious threats to the progress of mankind, however, is the activity of one particular syndicate about which little is known. This syndicate takes a page directly from the history of The War Years and peddles scientific secrets.

In our peaceful society of today, one would hardly suspect the existence of secret knowledge. During The War Years, it was understandable—the major powers each had their preciously guarded "military secrets" and scientific "hush-hush" projects. However, peaceful industry also has secrets: new processes, new developments, new products being prepared for the market. These secrets must be kept until they are in production and protected by International Patent laws.

It is the practice of the unknown syndicate to steal these industrial secrets and sell them illegally to the highest bidder. Unfortunately, not all industrial firms are honest; most of them do comply with local and international law, and are quite respectable in their businesses, since good business is largely good reputation and trustworthy contacts. But there are inevitably a few "bad apples" in the lot. Those few are directly responsible for the success of this syndicate, and it is they who sanction its crimes of theft of industrial secrets, kidnapping and coercion, and even murder of scientists and other people connected with such secrets...

Rourke tossed the book down and snapped on the screen almost as soon as the videophone chimes began ringing.

Gaines' beefy visage flashed on, its brow furrowed in sudden concern. "Mr. Rourke, there does seem to be trouble of some sort—"

"Spill it, man!" Rourke barked at him.

"Well, I called the guard posts and Martin Williams didn't answer," Gaines explained haltingly. "So I sent one of my relief men out to check on Williams. That was half an hour ago—"

"Where?"

"Over in the inertium gas plant. I'm on my way over there now, soon as I can get a squad together. Thought I'd call you and—"

"Get every man you have available," Rourke ordered crisply. "Sound the general alarm and alert all the other guard posts to trouble in the inertium plant building. I'll notify the Atom Town Police. Got that?"

GAINES was livid with excitement. "You—you think it's that serious?"

"My guess is sabotage! Now, hop to it, Gaines—" Rourke cleared the screen and dialed the Police. He gave a terse account to the uniformed Desk Sergeant, snapped off, and made a beeline out of his office for the airfield below.

The little field scooter was parked before the Control Tower as usual. He piled into it and swung it around, beading back from the field toward the sprawling plant buildings. He skidded along the dark, narrow alleyways between the buildings, tore madly across a broad parkway, and was skimming toward the looming, glass-walled hulk of the inertium gas-processing plant when he spotted Gaines and a platoon of uniformed plant guards marching over from the Main Gate. Marching! Why the devil weren't they double-timing over here?

He slammed on the brakes and squealed up to the plant's entrance on protesting tires. Leaping from the scooter, he ran up the steps to the dark portals and threw his weight against them.

They were locked.

He didn't have a key. Gaines' platoon was still too far away, still coming at a disciplined walk. Cursing under his breath, Rourke stumbled back down the steps and piled into the scooter. Throwing the gears in reverse, he backed up and swung around facing the steps. Then he gunned the turbine and the scooter hurtled forward.

It bounded up the steps and exploded through the entrance with a splintering crash. *That'll bring Gaines running!* Rourke thought, fighting the wheel to keep the little vehicle from careening against the walls of the dark, inner corridor. He caught a dim blur of movement to his left, and rolled out the side of the scooter onto the floor just as an orange streak of flame lighted the corridor. The loud blast of the shot followed it, and the bullet slammed into the opposite wall.

The scooter rolled ahead and crashed into the end of the corridor. Rourke came to his knees with a Luger in his fist and fired.

A dark figure slammed back against the wall, then pitched forward on its face.

Rourke climbed to his feet, breathing heavily, and moved down the corridor to the open doorway to the plant interior. He peeked cautiously around the edge of the doorway, then slipped through and let the blackness engulf him.

There was a dim gray light filtering in through the outer glass walls, but his drab gray attire rendered him invisible in it. He pulled his hat low over the white blob of his face and balanced a Luger pistol in each gray-gloved hand.

From here on it would be touch-and-go.

THE PLANT interior was three stories high, crammed with the dark bulks of giant tanks and a webwork of pipes, girders, and catwalks. He slipped silently through it, searching, and found what he was after near the center of the room. A dim blue glow, trickling from between the huge tanks. The tanks, he saw, formed a circular barricade around the spot. He faded into a nearby tangle of vertical pipes, found the rungs of a metal ladder, and began climbing upward.

He came out on a narrow catwalk high up near the ceiling and proceeded along it over the steel tops of the tanks until he was directly above the center of the room. Looking down, he saw four dark-garbed men wearing black masks and a uniformed plant guard standing in the blue glow of a lamp, their backs to each other as they peered around the tanks. A faint murmur of voices came drifting up to him.

It was too late to worry about exposing himself now. The five men below were prepared to fight to the finish. Other men would be killed.

But if none of the five escaped...

He lay down on the catwalk and extended his arm over the edge, pointing a Luger downward. Then he waited, a plan forming hurriedly in his mind. The Luger he aimed downward hadn't been fired yet.

Gaines' men came bursting into the building with a chorus of rebel yells and the echoing thunder of running feet.

The five men below hunched down behind their steel barricade and commenced firing. Other shots instantly replied. Bullets screamed and ricocheted in the dark metal catacombs.

With cool deliberation, Rourke fired five times, taking precise aim for each shot. The Luger threw ejected empty cartridges tinkling into the darkness below.

The five men sprawled grotesquely, their guns silent.

CHAPTER THREE
The Secret of AiRockets, Inc.

IT WAS a simple matter to slip down unseen from the upper catwalks in the noisy furor that followed—and to melt into the shadow of a wall air-vent, peeling out of his gray trench coat. He stuffed trench coat, hat, gloves and one Luger deep inside the air-vent, then took the other Luger—the one which had been fired only once—and slipped back out to the corridor.

He was crouching behind the twisted wreck of the little scooter, gun in hand, when the police arrived. Coming from the Administration Building, they used the same entrance he did.

They grabbed his Luger, slapped him around, and had the handcuffs snapped on his wrists before Gaines and the plant guards could arrive to explain who he was. The Sky Troopers were still suspicious until Detective Lieutenant Ybarra arrived and confirmed Rourke's identity. That satisfied them and they relaxed, letting Rourke go. Then only Ybarra was suspicious.

He looked at the body of the relief man Gaines had sent to check on Williams, noting its crushed skull with academic curiosity. Then he looked at the bodies of the five gunmen, Williams included. After that, he listened patiently through all the wildly conflicting stories told by Gaines' men, and the counter-claims they made as to who had accounted for which of the gunmen.

Then he took Rourke outside with him, alone. They climbed into a Police copter standing before the plant building and Ybarra took the controls, lifting it into the sky. "We're going over to the hangars," he explained curtly. "Your boss, McWilliams, is there with the men preparing your experimental craft for its test flight."

Rourke slumped back in the cushions and lit a cigarette. He blew smoke with a sigh of weariness, fully aware that Ybarra was watching him with narrowed interest."

"There is no family relationship between your boss McWilliams and this guard Williams who was working for the gunmen?" the suave Inspector asked suddenly.

Rourke looked honestly surprised. "None that I know of! Their names are just slightly similiar, that's all."

YBARRA nodded as if he had just learned something important. The police copter was creeping slowly over the plant buildings, taking its time about reaching the airfield.

"That was quite daring of you to go dashing over there with a gun in your hand," Ybarra commended gently. "And to smash the door down and shoot it out with one of them. You think they were hired to commit sabotage by Volks-Aero Industries, perhaps?"

"Who else?" Rourke protested. "After the threatening tone of that man, Czecmeloweicz—" He noted with quiet satisfaction that the name didn't upset the Inspector.

"Mr. McWilliams told me about that," Ybarra admitted readily. "And, of course, after what happened at the Simakov home, you had definite reason to suspect something like this would happen."

"What I can't understand is how Volks-Aero expected to get away with it," Rourke confessed worriedly.

"That's a good question," Ybarra agreed. "However, there's a more immediate question I would like to have answered." He turned his direct gaze on Rourke.

"What's that?"

"Do you have a permit for that gun?"

"As a matter of fact, I'm afraid I haven't." Rourke smiled lamely. "I kept it around the house, you see—"

"Yes." Ybarra's tone said he specifically did not see. "And then, how did you manage to kill the other five men? From the catwalk above? Each of them was shot from above, you know."

"Can you be sure of that?" Rourke spoke challengingly.

A faint smile quirked the corners of Ybarra's mouth. "No, I can't be sure. Men in a gun battle sometimes assume weird positions. However, I shall have that Luger of yours examined by ballistics, and a bullet from it will be compared with the bullets which killed those five men."

Rourke felt like grinning, but kept a straight face. *You'll have to find the other Luger to have the right gun, copper...*

"Have you nothing to say?" Ybarra goaded him.

Rourke shrugged resignedly. "I suppose you know what you're doing," he replied.

Ybarra's dark face twisted in disgust.

"SEVEN men killed!" the Old Man exclaimed bitterly. "Rourke, it's not going to help our company to be stained with blood."

They were standing together in the flood of light that spilled from the opened door of the giant hangar. There was Professor Thornton Weigand, a tall, skinny scarecrow with a shining bald dome and thick-lens spectacles, and husky, freckle-faced Skid Halloway, and a half-dozen engineers in white work coveralls. Old Man McWilliams stood in the center of the group, conversing with Rourke and Inspector Ybarra.

"It's not our fault any blood was spilled," Rourke replied grimly. "We're just protecting our interests, Mac."

"Gaines just called from the Main Gate," McWilliams retorted. "There's a crowd of reporters out there. What're you going to tell them?"

"*I'm* not going to tell them anything," Rourke said, then

tapped him on the chest. "*You're* going to tell them…"

"But, man, you're the hero of this skirmish. You blew in on those gunmen and held them at bay—"

"That's a matter of opinion." Rourke grinned. "But it won't do for me to go out there and tell them what a hero I am—you tell them."

"But we're running off this flight test."

"We can hold it a few minutes, boss," Halloway said.

Rourke nodded. "A few minutes. Fine—go talk to those reporters, Mac—just for a few minutes. Just long enough to tell briefly what a hero I am. Then say you have to get back here for the flight test."

McWilliams frowned and got a perplexed look on his face, then he nodded. "All right. What have you to say, Inspector Ybarra?"

"The case is closed for the moment, apparently," Ybarra replied. "The gunmen broke into your plant and your guards stopped them. We're taking out the bodies. However, I must ask Mr. Rourke not to take any sudden trips."

"Rourke?" McWilliams looked astonished.

"He was carrying a gun without a permit," Ybarra said, smiling. "Purely a piece of routine, Mr. McWilliams—we'll see to it that he actually gets a permit."

"Oh." The Old Man turned back to Rourke. "Any idea what the damage was to the plant?"

"Might've been some from the bullets—" Rourke caught himself; he had almost said *bouncing around in the works,* but remembered he wasn't supposed to have been inside the plant proper. Ybarra wouldn't have missed a slipup like that either.

McWilliams covered it up without the least knowledge that he did so. "Hang the bullets!" he exploded. "What'd those sneaky devils do to the plant?"

"I wouldn't know," Rourke answered truthfully. "Perhaps

we should ask Doc Simakov to come over and see what damage was done."

"Simakov? Why?"

"Because that's what they might've been after at his home," Rourke said. "They might've been looking for information that would tell them how to sabotage the inertium plant."

Ybarra looked suddenly thoughtful. "You know, Rourke, there might be something in that... Suppose I went after Dr. Simakov?"

"Later, Inspector," McWilliams vetoed. "No need to wake the man up this early. Bring him around after breakfast though, will you?"

"Let's shake on that." Ybarra stuck out his hand. "Can I give you a lift to the main gate in my copter, Mr. McWilliams?"

"If you will, yes." The Old Man shook hands with him, solemnly, then followed him out to the police copter.

Rourke stepped close to Skid Halloway. "If anybody wants me, I'll be in my office," he murmured.

Skid nodded.

Rourke borrowed another scooter from the hangar and drove off into the cool darkness. He shivered under his loose woolen blouse. Minutes later, he entered the Administration Building with a gray bundle under his arm. He carried it into his private office and stowed it in, the file-drawer of his desk—all but the Luger, which he reloaded and tucked into his trousers" waistband under the loose blouse.

Then he placed a call to United Air Delivery Service and got Manny on the screen. "How're things with you?" Manny asked.

"Had to clobber the lot of them," Rourke replied. "Covered my tracks, but Ybarra's suspicious as hell."

Manny grinned. "I'll arrange to have a private talk with

Ybarra. Don't worry about it. What's McWilliams doing about it?"

"He hasn't said, yet. But he'll probably fall for the game and place AiRockets under a tight security blanket."

"Volks-Aero gets the blame, huh?"

Rourke grinned at that. "I sort've suggested it myself."

"Good!" Manny gave an emphatic nod. "So long as they think we'll suspect Volks-Aero and not them, they'll think we're thrown off their trail—and they'll go ahead with this. I'll call you as soon as we get a line on anything."

"Right."

Rourke cleared the screen, noticed the seconds slipping past on the wall clock's face, and headed for the elevators in a run. He didn't want to miss Halloway's test flight.

THERE WERE three prototype models of the XR-1 sitting in the bright glare of the hangar lights. They were three fat, teardrop hulls squatting on the pudgy tires of their tricycle landing gear. Rourke paused in the shadows at the back of the hangar and watched the engineers swarm over the little craft, preparing them for flight.

Halloway would take one out for the test, and if it didn't check out he'd come back for another—and if it flunked out, he'd come back for the third. One out of three craft were favorable odds for providing a first-flight success. The faults in a ship that failed would be given careful study.

The ships had a sleek look in spite of their stubby proportions. Each fat hull was thirty feet long, with a blunt, pointed nose flaring back to a twelve-foot diameter at the center section, then tapering toward the tail where the rocket nozzle was mounted between four swept-back control fins. Glass blisters were mounted over their cabins, high on the elephantine back of the hulls.

Those cabins were sealed off from the rest of the hull,

Rourke knew. Each hull was actually no more than a rigid plastic shell. The engineers had the tail sections removed from the hulls now, and were draping the limp sealite balloon bladders into them. The bladders were clamped fast to the glittering cylinders of the atomic rocket units being slowly rolled forward. This was the real secret of the airockets, a thing Rourke understood only vaguely.

Simakov's synthetic inertium gas would freeze solid on an iron grid unless it were subjected to a temperature of thousands of degrees. Once subjected to such temperature, it became a stable gas—evaporating from the grid—having only a fraction of the mass of helium, with a proportionately larger "lifting capacity" per cubic foot.

Professor Weigand's atomic rocket unit used an atomic fuel without shedding any deadly radioactivity. It shielded its chain reaction with "force screens" built up between polar rods, and the emanations that escaped were far down in the infra-red band. The result was a concentrated point of thousands of degrees of heat. An iron grid had been mounted here, coated with Simakov's synthetic inertium solution. When the rocket began functioning, it "released" the inertium gas, which filled the bladder inside the hull and converted the ship into a lighter-than-air dirigible. The rocket delivered enough thrust, theoretically, to drive the ship at as much as five hundred miles per hour—or the nozzles could be opened, cutting down the thrust, and the ship could hover in midair.

There was no passenger discomfort from the rocket unit's tremendous heat production, since the inertium gas soaked the heat up quite efficiently. Refrigerating units took care of the difference.

Or so it said in the design specs.

It was Halloway's job to find out if it were true.

Halloway emerged from a locker room in the rear of the

hangar and came over to join Rourke. He wore a heavy, refrigerated suit of flight armor and carried a crash helmet under his arm.

"Thanks for the tip-off on checking these crates," he said gruffly. "We found the refrigerating units jammed on all three of them."

"Did you tell Mac?" Rourke asked. Skid nodded solemnly. "He didn't want to say anything in front of that police inspector, but we've got somebody right here in our research gang who's been selling us out. Nobody else would've known how to jam those refrigerating units!"

"How'd you spot them?"

"Ran a dye test—something we wouldn't have done normally." A wry grin creased Halloway's features. "Looks like it didn't do much good to risk our necks building that Lunar Base—we still got wars, anyway!"

"We've cut down the casualties, at least," Rourke replied gravely. "Seven dead is a lot better than seven million dead."

Skid raised his brows, then sighed and nodded agreement. "I guess it is at that. Thanks anyway, Tom."

"Sure," Rourke said.

HALLOWAY'S luck was with him. The first ship he chose passed the test successfully. They rolled it out on the field and he started up its rocket. It rested lightly on its tires as the gas expanded within its fat hull, then skittered forward gently as Skid applied flight thrust. He mastered its controls in a few minutes and soon had it skimming all over the field. Then he increased the thrust and lifted it easily into the calm, cool morning darkness.

The airocket had certain advantages not boasted by jetcopters. It had a speed range of five to 500 miles per hour; the jetcopter's range was only from five to 125. The airocket's range was an estimated five thousand miles without refueling; jetcopters could fly only a thousand miles nonstop. And an airocket could be flown in any and all weather; jetcopters still had to avoid areas where icing conditions prevailed.

Halloway brought the bullet-like craft screaming over the field, threw it into a tight turn, and came drifting down as lightly as a feather, the landing gear folding outward from the sleek hull. He clambered down the steps into the crowd of cheering, white-coveralled engineers.

Airockets were here to stay.

Rourke walked back to the Administration Building, picked up the gray bundle in his office, and carried it out to his copter in the parking lot. He flew home and deposited the trench coat and hat in his wardrobe closet, changed clothes, and got out a spare Luger pistol to complete his usual armament. Then he joined the traffic patterns and windmilled into Atom Town for breakfast. Dawn was exploding its brilliant colors in the east.

He parked the copter on a roof and descended the elevator into a brightly-lighted roboteria. He slid into a booth seat and a small metal monster rolled up on silent casters to accept his order. He gave it, then plunked change into the coin slot and had a morning paper plopped out to him from the wall panel.

The story had crowded even the news of the expedition on Mars from the front page. Headlines shouted in bold black type: AIROCKETS STOP SABOTEURS. There was even a fairly handsome photo of him, one he recognized as having been given to Miss Dorothea Finch, his secretary, after persistent requests for it. The write-up gave him credit for spearheading the plant guards' attack on the saboteurs, smashing in the plant doors with a scooter, and there was a somewhat heroic fiction about his facing the saboteurs' blazing guns single-handed until the guards arrived.

And then they went into the story of how he'd saved the lives of Doctor Simakov and his daughter from the same gang of killers. This, being continued on the inside pages, sported a fetching glamour photo of Miss Roberta Simakov—and directly across from her was an even more fetching photo of Miss Dorothea Finch in a tape sunsuit! Both were identified with broad implications in the solid-type captions below the photos. Rourke pursed his lips and gave a long, low whistle. The robot brought his order and he settled down to breakfast.

AIR TRAFFIC had begun to thicken with office people coming to work when he emerged on the roof landing again. He received several startled glances when he stopped at a newsstand and bought a copy of *Spaceways*, but managed to slip away and get off in his copter without attracting too much attention.

He returned to his office, sat down with the magazine, and proceeded to read it from cover to cover. It was the logical thing to do if he were to write an article on airockets for the magazine. He should know something about the general atmosphere of the stories and articles it featured.

Spaceways was a fairly good general slick magazine; though it specialized in the field of science fiction. The articles were clear, concise and to the point, dealing more with what the subjects meant to the reader than with technical information on the subjects. The stories ranged all the way from satirical humor to psychological tragedy to a suspenseful adventure serial. The back pages of the magazine were healthfully loaded with full color advertisements of wall televisions, jetcopters, electronic appliances and house robots, and world airline tourist attractions.

He was aboard the Space Admiral's flagship off Cygnus Major, watching that austere gentleman direct a battle fleet against the enemy *Ulthii* forces via telepathic commands, when the door opened and Miss Finch waltzed in. She swayed up to the desk, smiling, and laid a glossy photograph before him. It was an exact copy of the one featured in the morning papers, tape sunsuit and all.

"I thought you might like it," she purred musically.

IT WAS three days before he heard from Manny again. Inspector Ybarra dropped by to return his Luger with a gun permit made out for it. McWilliams told him that company security was being tightened up, and uniformed plant guards checked him in and out of the parking lot every day. Doc Simakov came, inspected the inertium plant, and left AiRockets' engineers to clear up the minor damage. Halloway took the experimental ships up with increasing frequency, testing the bugs out of them for the flight engineers. Miss Finch whistled every time Rourke passed through the outer office. Her photograph won prominent display on his desk. A Cantonese interpreter in San Francisco gave him half-a-day's argument over the wording of an advertisement for a Chinese magazine.

Manny called on the afternoon of the third day. The cloud doctors of Weather Control had been up to their usual tricks and the rain was pouring down outside.

"I got news," Manny said.

"Oh, fine," Rourke groaned. "I'm expected for dinner at the Simakov's tonight."

"Well, la-de-*dah!*" Manny snorted derisively. "Give the princess my love, your highness."

"Okay, okay," Rourke protested. "Let's have it, slave driver."

"We almost have the complete data on the syndicate," Manny said. His gaze was coldly impersonal.

Rourke let the words sink in, then leaned back and cupped

his chin in his hand. "Let's hear it," he prompted.

"We caught the key factor as soon as the newspapers reported that fracas you had at AiRockets," Manny complied evenly. "Our boy Czecmeloweicz left the Hotel Atometro looking unhappy. He met Betty Lou Johnson in a roboteria and they had a lengthy conversation—"

He left the screen, then returned with a typed report sheet in his hand. "Our lip reader says they wondered if you were a World Police Inspector. You've succeeded too well in wrecking their plans, it seems. Czecmeloweicz suspects you, but Miss Johnson doesn't—so Czecmeloweicz ordered her to check up on you personally.

"Then Czecmeloweicz sent off a cablegram to Budapest. We got the address and tipped off World Police Frankfurt. They took it from there, and now we know the boss of the syndicate is a man called Paulas Cretius—tall, slender build, silvery hair, immaculate in appearance, face deeply lined with ruddy complexion and deep-set, baggy blue-green eyes; six feet and a hundred and eighty pounds, from fifty to seventy years old with excellent health. This Cretius is on his way here via stratoliner right now."

"WE'VE SMOKED out the boss-man, eh?" Rourke grinned. "More than that," Manny replied emotionlessly. "Paulas Cretius cabled an address in Mexico City; World Police Havana checked on it. There's a gang of killers due in here tomorrow at noon. Cretius is going to give us a battle." He paused, laying the report sheet aside.

"But the weak link was Czecmeloweicz," he went on. "Frankfurt checked Budapest on him, finally traced him to Warsaw. The Czecmeloweicz family is in building construction there; they recognized this crook's photostat. Seems he worked for them once as a young man—his name was Jan Lipenchek then—and tried a little embezzlement. He served a nine-year prison term for that. Then his criminal record extends over most of Eastern Europe. We've tied him in with Paulas Cretius and, by checking what little is known of their movements, we have a fair outline of the history of this syndicate."

"So Czecmeloweicz is Jan Lipenchek," Rourke mused grimly. "He should've chosen a more untraceable name for his *nom de guerre*—like Schmidt."

"We have the complete pattern of data to compute this, except for one factor," Manny said. "We haven't figured Betty Lou Johnson into this deal. We can't calibrate her."

"That shouldn't be too difficult."

"Oh, come now! You *are* young, aren't you? That little babe is probably the toughest nut in the whole outfit, sonny."

"What do Headquarters' technicians say?" Rourke asked.

"They say we either take Miss Johnson out of circulation—and that'll tip Cretius off to us for sure—or we let her go to work on you and lose a promising young inspector." Manny was watching him critically. "It's up to you, Tom."

"Let 'er rip," Rourke said. "I'll see if I can't come out alive."

"If you're killed, that'll give us enough to calibrate Miss Johnson into the equation," Manny informed him cryptically. "If you aren't killed, bring us a calibration. Good hunting."

The screen went blank.

"OH, HELLO, Rourke!" Professor Weigand exclaimed, coming forward across the Simakovs' living room. "Didn't know you'd be here. This is an unexpected pleasure, young man."

Rourke smiled and shook hands with the Professor as Robbie Simakov clung affectionately to his arm. "Mr. Rourke is my guest tonight, Professor Weigand," she announced, with a slight grin of mischief.

"Oh?" Weigand chuckled graciously. "Well, I must congratulate you upon your good taste, my dear. He is a handsome devil, isn't he?"

Rourke took their ribbing with a good-natured shrug and went on to greet Dr. Simakov. "Good to have you here, Rourke," the little gray-haired scientist welcomed him. "Drinks before dinner? Martini? I mix a special one."

"I could do with a special one," Rourke accepted gladly.

They chatted over drinks for a while, Weigand giving them a general rundown on the successful test-flights of the airockets, and then entered the warm gloom of the dining room, where gold trim winked on rich mahogany paneling and silverware glittered brightly in the glow of tapered candles.

Conversation at dinner was led mostly by the two scientists, with lean-faced Professor Weigand bobbing his shiny bald dome as he waxed enthusiastic about his airockets. They would never do for heavy shipping or freight transportation, he explained, because the power necessary for that was greater and costlier than the power used if the conventional atomic-turbine ocean liners and freighters. However, as a private passenger craft, the airocket's fast speed and five-thousand-mile range would promote more world travel than ever before.

Americans hadn't yet grown accustomed to taking a trip to Asia for a pleasant weekend, or the Asiatics to America! Few people would consider a trip to Europe merely an overnight business trip, done in one's own privately flown ship.

Airockets would make such things commonplace. The result would be to increase peoples' knowledge and understanding of each other, making for a more tolerant and good humored world civilization. Rourke caught the trend in this direction and went off in a spiel about his worldwide advertising campaign, and how widely ordinary business practices varied in different parts of the world; and how tough it was sometimes to understand these local ways of doing business and comply with them as prescribed by international law.

He immediately was trounced by two scientists who eagerly explained that the ways of conducting scientific research were the same, no matter where you were...

ROBBIE came to his rescue and dragged him into the living room, leaving the two elderly men to their pipes and coffee and technological progress.

"When Father argues with you," she remarked, half-smiling, "it means you've won his unquestioning approval."

"He should be more careful," Rourke taunted her. "I have a few secrets which might seem highly unquestionable."

She laughed appreciatively, pulling him across the room to the couch. "I'm not sure. I could resent that," she murmured, as they sat down beside each other. "But then, I'm not sure I understand what you meant by it, either."

Rourke stared into the glowing crystals of the electronic fireplace. "I'd be glad to discuss that," he said. "But it happens they're right in the next room and might be coming in here any minute..." He stifled an after-dinner yawn behind his hand.

"Well." Robbie sat back and smiled. She was wearing a rich crimson gown of synthetic material that molded like film to her firm body.

Rourke felt butterflies cruising inside him. "Are you always this...beautiful?"

"Uh-uh..." She shook her head impishly. "Only on special occasions. Like, for instance, when a man is around." She leaned forward and picked a cigarette from the silver tray on the low glass-topped table. "Were you ever married,

Tom?"

He held the table lighter aflame for her. "Not that I recall," he answered musingly. "Have you?"

She looked up at him, then blew a smoke ring that encircled his nose. "No, I haven't. And with you? It's never been the right person, has it?"

"For one reason or another, no—it never has." He set the lighter on the table, then settled back beside her and put his arm around her. She snuggled in closer, resting against him.

"Tell me about yourself," she murmured.

Rourke gazed at the fireplace glow. Bright crystals, activated to a flaming glow of heat by electronic current.

"Well?" she prompted.

"I...was born in Singapore," he began haltingly. "I grew up in the Canadian Northwest—my father was an engineer in foreign employment. I studied at the University of Brazil, lived like a starving rat in the slums of Paris, became lieutenant of a band of Arab bandits, was carried half-dead of thirst off the Gobi Desert—"

"Oh, all right!" She pulled away from him, indignantly. "I didn't think that newspaper publicity would go to your head..."

"But it's true," he protested.

"Shall we see what's on television?" She rose and stalked across the room.

HE WAS flying his copter homeward when he reached under the seat and took his guns and shoulder holsters from a small compartment. He slipped out of his jacket and buckled the guns on.

The videophone chimed softly.

He struggled back into his jacket, hurriedly, and pulled the screen mount up over his lap. The screen flashed onto the moonlit interior of another copter and a tall, blonde girl who smiled at him. "You're Tom Rourke, aren't you!" she exclaimed.

"That's right," he admitted.

"Thought I recognized you as you flew past me a moment ago. I'm just above and behind you now." Her voice was grave and sweet. "Sorry to bother you this way, but they say you're a brave man, Mr. Rourke. And I'm in trouble—"

"What sort of trouble?"

"I'm mixed up with the gang that tried to sabotage your company several nights ago," she replied frankly. "I'm afraid they're trying to kill me, Mr. Rourke."

"Give me your name," Rourke said.

"Betty Lou Johnson."

"All right, Miss Johnson. Why aren't you going to the police?"

"Prison would be preferable to dying," she retorted. "But I don't want to go to prison either, if I can help it. I'd rather come to you."

Her copter was moving alongside his now. Rourke gazed out at it, with its blue nightlight glowing atop the teardrop hull and its whirling rotors shimmering in the moonlight. They glided along smoothly over the black earth where the warm lights of homes were scattered coals of some giant's fire. Thunderclouds hovered ahead and to the right, with blurred sheets of rain descending from them. A bright tongue of lightning flickered near the horizon.

She started out with a lie! Rourke thought. He'd passed no other copters in the traffic patterns since leaving the Simakov home. So that meant he had been watched, and she'd been informed when he left and which direction he flew—she would have had to have known that in order to be able to intercept him. That meant a dark figure lurking out beyond the clumps of cactus, watching the Simakov home, plotting the course of his copter as he flew away from it.

Miss Johnson had not fallen out with her gang.

"All right, Miss Johnson. I'm willing to talk to you. Suppose you lead the way?"

"There's a place near the spaceport where we can talk," she said, easing her copter ahead of his to lead him there...

THE NEVADA spaceport was a broad expanse of flat, level field ten miles south of Atom Town. Its edge was lined with giant, hangar-like buildings and terraced rows of workshops, laboratories, factories and warehouses. The whole establishment was fenced off and guarded by uniformed troopers of the United Nations Armed Forces.

Beyond the fence was a wild collection of hotels, restaurants, bars, and ramshackle plastiform houses, with field scooters scurrying about on the dirt streets. Garish neon lights flickered dimly through a dark curtain of rain as Betty Lou Johnson swooped her copter low over the settlement. She settled down on a small parking roof and Rourke jockeyed his ship into the narrow space left behind her. A brilliant red sign flashed on and off, wetly proclaiming SPACEPORT MOTEL to the rain-drenched night.

Rourke unzipped his jacket and unfastened the holster from beneath his right armpit, quickly storing it in the little compartment beneath the seat. Then he zipped up his jacket and climbed out into the soaking downpour. Betty Lou came tripping back from her ship to join him, her blonde hair plastered down over her forehead.

"Come on!" she yelled. "This way!"

They ran through the rain to the doorway of an elevator shaft. She huddled against him in the small chamber, her short dress clinging wetly to her skin, and pressed the main floor button. "We'll go to my apartment and talk," she said, as the elevator descended. "You don't mind, do you?"

"Not when you stand this close," he replied softly.

She looked up at him, then turned and slid a caressing hand over his chest. Then she scowled at him. "You've got a gun!"

"The police gave me a permit for one." He pulled out his billfold and showed her the permit.

They left the elevator and strode along covered walks past a row of dark, rain-shrouded bungalows until she turned in to one and slid a key into the lock. She led him inside and snapped on the light, revealing a small, cozy bedroom-living room. She closed the door behind him and locked it, then came up to him and slipped her arms around his neck.

"I don't mind the gun," she murmured against his lips. "I want you to help me, so I'm going to be nice to you." The kiss was long, full-lipped, and clinging.

He had been neatly maneuvered so he was facing the closet door across the room. The door was opened a crack and the toe of a foot was visible in the blackness beyond it. The toe of a man's boot, large size.

She released him and stepped back, her firm breasts heaving against the taut, wet dress as she regained her breath. She smiled bewitchingly, then slowly followed his stare down at herself.

"Sit down," she said softly. "I'll get undressed."

Rourke moved over to the one comfortable chair in the room and sat down. She swayed past him, her hand gliding over his cheek in a damp caress. The whispery sounds of wet cloth came from behind him.

Then the closet door exploded inward. Two men piled out, cursing. One was as big as an Indian wrestler. The other held a gun.

CHAPTER FOUR
The Crime Machine

IT WAS quite a spectacle when the two Sky Troopers burst through the front door and came charging into the room, guns drawn.

Rourke was flattened across the bed, his clothes torn, and his face beaten to the consistency of raw hamburger.

The skinny little runt with the wizened face was cowering in the corner, clutching his shattered right arm. A bullet from Rourke's Luger had done that. His shiny, nickel-plated revolver was lost somewhere in the general wreckage of the room.

A huge, gorilla-like figure was sprawled on its face in the middle of the floor. There were six neat bullet holes in its back, also contributed by Rourke's Luger—though he hadn't been holding it at the time. The giant bruiser had reached him before he could fire.

The Luger itself lay on the floor next to the bed. Just over it, and on the bed, sat Betty Lou Johnson. She was on her knees and had Rourke's head pillowed on her lap. She was wiping at his face with a wet dress, and the tears were pouring down her cheeks and splashing on him. She was stark naked, her shoulders twitching as harsh sobs tore at her throat.

"You're just a nice guy!" she was saying, over and over. *"You're just a nice guy!"*

The cops left them alone. One picked up the Luger and another went to call Police headquarters in Atom Town.

News photographers and telecast cameramen were crowded around outside when Rourke was carried out. Betty Lou followed, bundled in a policeman's raincoat.

Then Rourke was alone, lying on a stretcher inside a police ambulance copter. He wondered why it didn't take off.

Then a white-uniformed, attractive nurse was slipping into the seat beside him, and a taller, darker form climbed in behind her. It bent over, and Ybarra's hard, dark features floated above him.

"How do you feel, Rourke?"

Rourke moved his puffed lips and winced at a stab of pain.

"Not like talking, eh? I don't blame you. Nice girls you shack up with fella—only this one had a wrestler for a boyfriend."

IT WAS all over the newspapers. The story was exactly as Ybarra had framed it, with added references to the broad, romantic implications the newspapers had voiced earlier. One paper daringly placed three photographs together— Robbie Simakov's glamour photo, Dorothea Finch's cheesecake photo, and a shot of the naked Miss Betty Lou Johnson with a policeman's raincoat pulled around her.

Rourke was definitely the Gay Lothario.

He was propped up in the hospital bed reading a dog-eared copy of *Spaceways* when Miss Finch visited him.

"Are you all right?" she asked, standing beside the bed.

"I'm fine," he said. "How are things at the office?"

"We'll manage," She was twisting a tiny handkerchief to shreds. "The papers say you'll be tried for shooting that man."

"In self defense." He nodded stiffly. "The district attorney assured me yesterday that it will merely be a formality. I won't even have to appear in court."

"That girl—"

"She'll have to appear for killing that other fellow, but they tell me she'll get only a light sentence."

He was allowed to go home a week later. He was delivered to his doorstep in a police copter and escorted into his own living room by Detective Lieutenant Ybarra.

Manny was sitting in the chair next to the television set. "Hail the conquering hero," he greeted sarcastically. "You broke the camel's back for us, son. Little Betty Lou poured her heart out to Lieutenant Ybarra here, who naturally told it to us."

"My men rounded up that gang of Mexican killers and shipped them back to Mexico," Ybarra added, helping Rourke into a chair.

Rourke looked up at him. "So that's why nothing's happened. You pulled Cretius' muscle-boys out from under him!"

Manny nodded affirmatively. "Looks like it's up to Cretius and his pal Lipenchek to pull this job alone now— unless they put it off until more help can arrive. Their other gangs are all in Europe though."

"You're watching them, aren't you?"

"Not after little Betty Lou spilled the beans..." Manny gave him a wry grin. "They knew she'd talked as soon as Ybarra's men closed in on their Mexican gang. Those two vanished like puffs of smoke when that happened."

Rourke grunted. He knew that no one could keep watching a skillful crook who didn't want to be watched; there were too many ingenious ways to shake a follower and fade into the crowd. "But we've computed all the factors in this case now, haven't we?" he asked.

"Everything," Manny agreed.

"Have Headquarters' Technicians passed on it for the brain?"

"The brain can take it," Manny confirmed. "And it's time we used the brain. I've got your wall television rigged up here for it." He looked meaningfully at Ybarra. "You'll have to leave us, Lieutenant. Regulations, you know."

Ybarra bared his teeth in a smile and strode quietly out.

CRIME was an equation.

When the equation was complete, the sum of its factor described the negative force of evil in human society with the cold logic of mathematical accuracy.

Mathematically, the one way to cancel out a negative force was to oppose it with an equal positive force. So you drew up your equation for crime, added an equal sign, and drew a question mark on the other side of the equal sign.

Negative crime equals positive what? Find the answer, and crime can be cancelled out.

Manny put a sealed-beam call through to the United Nations Center in New York. There, in a subterranean room with banks of winking signal lights covering the walls, a staff of white-coated Technicians went into action. Manny watched them on the wall screen in Rourke's living room, shuffling a pile of report sheets on his lap and comparing data with the Chief Technician.

Beyond the walls of blinking lights, buried deep in the solid rock of Manhattan Island, a giant electronic computer hummed and chicked and chuttered, snicking relays and flashing tubes as the data were fed into it.

All the factors of the equation were coded to the computer's language. The case histories of Paulas Cretius and Jan Lipenchek, alias Czecmeloweicz; the vague knowledge of all the past activities of their world crime syndicate; the known crimes which had been committed, circumstantially attributable to this syndicate. They included the computer's previous answer—that AiRockets, Inc., would be a victim of the syndicate—and a complete resume of what had happened from the day Rourke joined AiRockets up to the present moment. And then they threw in the equal sign.

Negative crime equals positive what?

And they waited. The day was past by then, and evening shadows were lengthening under the trees beyond the living room's transparent outer wall. Rourke had his house robot rustle them up some food.

The brain solved it. Analyzing, scrutinizing, weighing in balance, it came up with an answer. The brain could do it—had done it for years. Crime was the one form of human endeavor capable of being broken down into logical components. The human mind was incredibly complex, far beyond the abilities of a man-made machine to compute; but human habit patterns fell into a definite category that characterized Man as an animal. And crime was a habit. Crooks habitually frequented the same haunts used the same aliases, retained the same methods in their work throughout their lives, even though those habits repeatedly led to their apprehension by the police. The brain could compute crime. So it gave them an answer.

And the answer was completely useless.

"The leader of the world crime syndicate in question," said the Chief Technician, reading from the spool-tape just torn from the computer's slot, "is World Police Inspector Thomas Rourke:"

ROURKE? They were all staring at him—the men on the screen and Manny seated beside him. There was a glint of amusement in their eyes.

"Run it through again," Manny said. "We'll get the same answer," the Chief Technician protested.

"Wait…" Rourke spoke calmly.

"We'll take our equation a step further. Include this factor: I deny that I'm the leader of the world crime syndicate."

The Chief Technician nodded. "We'll include that factor, Inspector."

They ran it through again. The brain chittered and clucked and flashed lights and flickered tubes. They waited.

The shadows outside deepened into twilight. The courses of a half-dozen stars across the Universe would have been easier to compute than the problem the brain was solving.

Then an alarm gong clanged and the spool-tape spewed from the slot.

The Chief Technician picked it up and translated its cryptic markings.

"Data are insufficient," he said.

"But that's impossible!" Manny jumped to his feet angrily. "We've dug out every single factor concerning this case—"

"Then the brain wouldn't give us this answer," the Chief Technician reproved him. "After all, Inspector, the brain is designed—"

"I know, I know." Manny waved him down. "And it's no smarter than the men who run it. I don't—mean you, either—I mean me! I'm the one who collected this data."

"Then there's just one solution," the Chief Technician advised him. "You'll have to wait for some further development in your case and present it again, with that development included."

"Suppose we do that now?" Rourke asked.

Manny whirled to him. "What's on your mind, Tom?"

"The way it accused me of being the leader of the syndicate," Rourke admitted honestly. "I'm wondering how it reached that conclusion."

"We could check back through it and give you the answer in about forty years," the Chief Technician answered, grinning.

Rourke shook his head. "No, I don't mean how the brain got it. I'm wondering what factors *lead* to it, the factors that we *stuck into the brain.*"

"You mean it's something we have right at our fingertips? Something we should've seen and included in the equation?" Manny queried.

"That's exactly what I mean. Now, if I were the leader of the syndicate, what would I be doing now?"

Manny peered at him narrowly. "You'd be wondering how you could make contact with Cretius and Lipenchek to get this job done."

"I'd probably have taken care of that before I left the hospital, wouldn't I?"

"Probably."

"Then right now I'd be planning where to strike next," Rourke continued. "And where would I strike? Right where AiRockets, Incorporated keeps the technical data on their secret, the inertium gas and atomic rocket unit."

Manny nodded and licked his lips. "All right. Where do they keep it?"

"I don't know," Rourke confessed. "But old man McWilliams knows, and so does Professor Weigand. So suppose I ask them?"

"You'd need a reason for asking, wouldn't you?"

"I've been risking my neck for that company, haven't I? What more reason would I need? I'd say I'm curious about this thing I've been protecting so heroically. I'd like to see the blueprints on it and have Prof. Weigand explain them to me."

"So you'd call Weigand!" Manny concluded.

"So I'll *call* Weigand." Rourke climbed stiffly out of his chair and crossed the room to the videophone.

THE FIRST words Professor Thornton Weigand uttered as his image flashed on the screen sent a shock tingling down to the base of Rourke's spine.

"Why, hello there, Tom!" he exclaimed jovially. "I've been expecting you to drop in any minute now."

"Drop in?" Rourke echoed faintly. "Prof—who told you I was going to drop in?"

"Why, your secretary…Miss Finch. She told me all about your detective work with Lieutenant Ybarra and the Police in rounding up that gang of Mexican saboteurs," Weigand chuckled wryly. "Quite a trick, getting that Johnson girl to side with you against the crooks. I'd like to hear about it—"

"Miss Finch gave you all the details, eh?"

"Why—why, yes. Shouldn't she?" Weigand was taken aback. "Sorry—I mean, if those newspaper stories were to hide anything—you haven't told Miss Simakov, have you? She's rather upset!"

"I'll call her—"

"Let me do that." Weigand smiled. "You come on over—I have the blueprints here to show you."

"I'll be there, and…Weigand?"

"Yes?"

"Be careful. You're in more danger now than you ever were…" Rourke flicked off the screen and hurried back to Manny.

"I heard it, Tom," Manny said. "We'll enter Miss Finch in on the computation. If they get the blueprints from Weigand, this is strictly our case—you know that, don't you?"

Rourke nodded, limping toward the door. "Call my copter when the brain has its answer," he said, then he stepped into the foyer. Opening a small wall panel, he took out a holstered .50-caliber Browning machine pistol and buckled it on—strictly heavy artillery. But the time had come for it. He limped out of the house and hauled himself into his jetcopter, then sent it hurtling up into the night.

The little copter poised in the black night on thrumming rotors. It was one of those calm, chilly nights without a moon, when the sky seemed a deep shadow filled with the twinkling motes of stars and the ground below was a vague blackness with the warm sparks of house lights scattered thinly over it.

ROURKE remembered that Professor Weigand had a small home southeast of Atom City, and headed his copter that way while unfolding the videophone screen. He called AiRockets and got Gaines, on duty at the Main Gate, to look up the Professor's exact address for him. Gaines had it for him in forty seconds. Rourke switched off the screen and folded the videophone back into its niche, then slowed his speed and studied the black earth below, picking out the bright red traffic-lane arrows. He read his position from their numbers, checked his panel map, and corrected his course.

It took him down along the outskirts of the spaceport. He muttered a curse as red-green blinker lights warned him to detour away from the spaceport field. He swerved farther east and gazed out to the right toward the glow of floodlights that marked the field. The tall, shimmering needle of an S-90 Earth-Moon supply ship stood poised on its tail fins in the center of the field, preparing for takeoff.

Weigand's home was nestled on the slope of a low line of hills, east of the spaceport. Rourke set his copter neatly onto the landing ramp beside the dark house and unfastened the flap on his holster as he strode across to the portico entrance. If Weigand were waiting for him, why was the house in darkness?

He stepped into the deep shadow of the portico and felt along the wall for the doorbell. A faint sound behind him snapped his nerves tense, and he started to whirl—

A hard object grazed the back of his head and slammed into the base of his neck. Pinwheels of pain exploded in his mind and the floor came up to flatten his face.

He heard dim footsteps fading into the darkness in a stumbling run.

It had been a downward blow. If it had been swung squarely against his neck, the blow would have broken his neck.

But someone had swung at his head. And missed.

He began to feel the cold floor pressing against him. The fall had broken open a few scabs on his face; he could feel the trickle of blood. He was anxiously aware that only a few seconds had passed.

He rolled to his hands and knees and lunged out from the portico, clawing the heavy, compact Browning machine pistol from its holster.

He saw his assailant, then, running with a stooped stagger across the landing ramp. Heading for his copter, Rourke could see that the man was tall and slender, with silvery hair, and a gun glinted in his hand. He was running stooped over, with an arm clamped around his middle.

"Hold it, Cretius!" Rourke yelled.

Paulas Cretins skidded to a halt. He turned, weaving on his feet, and lifted his gun. Its muzzle winked flame and its sharp bark echoed into the darkness. The bullet smacked the wall behind Rourke and *squee-e-ed* off to the right.

ROURKE brought up his Browning and squeezed the trigger. The bulky gun bucked and roared yammeringly in his fist, spitting orange tongues of flame against the night. Ejected cartridges tinkled musically at his feet.

Cretius was hurled backward by the impact of the burst. His upper body folded over as if there were a hinge in his chest, then he smacked the ramp, skidding, and sprawled lifeless.

Rourke walked slowly out to him and stood over him, then kneeled down beside him. The man's eyes were wide open, glistening in the starlight. Blood spurted from his mouth as his lips worked, trying to form words. Finally, the words were coughed out.

"Trixie Finch—double-crossed—"

Rourke reached out and grasped the arm clamped over Cretius' stomach, ignoring the now-dead eyes and the gory mass of the chest. He tugged at the frozen arm, prying it away from the dead man's middle. He gazed for a long moment at the small, neat hole that had been covered by the arm. It was a small-caliber hole.

Someone else had shot Cretius in the stomach.

Trixie Finch! Double-crossed.

"Trixie" Finch—Miss Dorothea Finch. Rourke released the stiff, cramped arm and rose. His neck was numb.

Then he walked back to the portico entrance. No need to bother with the doorbell now; he pushed against the front door and swung it open, stepping into the pitch-blackness within.

He felt his way cautiously across the foyer, fumbled along the wall with his fingertips until he found the doorway into the living room, then slipped through and stopped cold.

It was a broad, spacious living room, with a transparent outer wall that curved gracefully around to give a full view of the wide valley and the distant spaceport field, where the tall needle of the Earth-Moon supply ship gleamed in the glow of floodlights.

As Rourke slipped through the door, his attention was immediately caught by that scene. The field floodlights had gone out.

The next instant, a blinding white blaze exploded beneath the Earth-Moon ship's tail. It heaved itself up from the field and went climbing up into the night sky, a pillar of dazzling fire pouring from its rockets.

The bright reflection of that fire illuminated the broad living room. It revealed the twisted figure lying beside an overturned chair. It showed Rourke, in that brief instant, that the shiny bald head had been shattered like a ripe melon.

Then the illumination flickered and died. The S-90 supply

ship was gone into outer space.

A faint, echoing blowtorch roar came drifting through the night.

Rourke strode over to the wall-switch and flipped on the lights.

THERE WAS a wide folding-table set in the middle of the living room. The table's surface was conspicuously bare.

Cretius and "Trixie" Finch—and possibly Jan Lipenchek—had been here. Miss Finch had managed to get them in without arousing Professor Weigand's suspicions. Then Weigand had been murdered. The blueprint designs of the airocket were swept off the folding-table and folded up to be taken out to a waiting copter.

But two's company, perhaps, and three's a crowd. Now that they had the airocket secret, somebody decided they didn't have to deal Paulas Cretius in on it. So they dealt him out—with a bullet in his stomach—and left him behind...

It was possible that "Trixie" Finch thought more of Lipenchek than she did of Cretius. Cretius had been an elderly man. An attractive young girl could get bored with an elderly man after living with him for a while. Miss Finch probably lived with him in Europe before she came to join AiRockets, Inc., as a secretary.

This deduction was very probably true, Rourke knew.

Then he was whirling across the room to flatten against the wall, his Browning held ready.

Light, swift footsteps came tripping through the outer foyer.

Miss Roberta Simakov ran into the room, her features pallid with shock. She froze in her tracks and gave a sharp gasp as she saw Weigand's body.

Rourke breathed a sigh of relief, sagging back against the wall. The faint sound made her whirl like a suddenly released spring. She stared at him, wide-eyed and expressionless, her mouth gaping open. She saw the ugly bulk of the Browning machine pistol in his hand.

Then she screamed. And screamed. Backing away from him in terror!

Rourke jammed the Browning into its holster and strode across the room. He slapped her hard, first with one hand, then the other. She collapsed into his arms in a dead faint.

Rourke picked her up and carried her out of the house, his blood-streaked face set in a grim mask. He carried her over to his jetcopter and shoved her into the seat, then crawled in beside her and lifted the little craft into the dark sky. The cold night wind came sweeping in through the panels, which he had left open deliberately, and Roberta stirred feebly against him. He pushed her over into the corner of the seat and was rewarded by a fearful intake of breath as she regained consciousness. She stared at him in wide-eyed fright.

"Why—why did you do it, Tom?" The words slurred through her twisted lips. "That—woman! And now murder!"

"Shut up!" Rourke ordered gruffly.

He ignored her, setting the controls and pulling the videophone up over his lap. The call-chimes were ringing faintly. He flipped on the screen.

"Tom, you all right?" Manny's face was taut with concern. "I've been trying to get you for the past five minutes!"

ROURKE winced as the copter wallowed through an air pocket. He fought down the nausea in his stomach. His head felt like a balloon with the dull pain throbbing up from his neck. "I've been busy," he said, then related what had happened in terse, clipped phrases.

Manny nodded. "You'd better get over to AiRockets, Incorporated. We've got the answer—"

"What about Miss Simakov?"

"Ask her why she was there."

Rourke turned to her. She was gazing at the tiny screen in puzzlement. "Why did you come over to Weigand's tonight?" he asked her.

Her eyes flicked up to his face. "I...Professor Weigand called me...asked me to come over. He said he had something to tell me—about you!" She spat the word with scornful disgust.

"He wanted to tell you I was working with the police," Rourke explained dryly. He turned back to the screen. "I'll take her with me to the company. But why AiRockets?"

"According to the brain, that's where they're headed—if they haven't already arrived there! I've alerted the plant guards out there." Manny left the screen and returned holding a sheet of notepaper. "Here's the answer the brain gave us, after we included your secretary in the equation:

" 'Miss Dorothea Finch has been taking calls regularly from Jan Lipenchek, alias Czecmeloweicz. World Police agents watching Lipenchek were not suspicious because it was assumed Lipenchek would call AiRockets from time to time, trying to persuade the company to accept the fake offer from Volks-Aero. Lipenchek always called Miss Finch at the company; she took the calls without Rourke's knowledge.

" 'Her purpose inside the company was to find the location of the blueprint designs for the airocket, and to inform Lipenchek on what success he had in diverting suspicion to the Volks-Aero firm.

" 'She failed to locate the blueprints. Her boss, Rourke, had broken up the gang's attacks on Dr. Simakov and the company's inertium gas plant; she began to suspect that Rourke was a World Police Inspector and that he knew her true identity as well. Through Lipenchek, she had Miss Betty Lou Johnson approach Rourke and try to expose him. Sure that she was right, she personally contacted other members of the gang and had them catch Rourke with Miss Johnson and beat him to death. Rourke played innocent, even refusing to use his judo training in the resulting fistfight until it was almost too late. But Miss Johnson was convinced he wasn't a cop, and rescued him. Miss Finch had also been planning to double cross Paulas Cretius and had persuaded Jan Lipenchek to help her. Using her position as Rourke's secretary, she will arrange with Prof. Weigand to have the airocket plans at his home, ostensibly to show them to Rourke—' "

Manny broke off. "The brain went on to predict just about what happened out there, as far as the crooks are concerned. Then it wraps the case up with this: 'Miss Finch and Lipenchek will attempt to steal an airocket from the company and fly it to Mexico. With the experimental airocket and the plans, they can get other engineers to build airockets illegally, which they will sell through the syndicate to other criminal groups for inflated prices. The airockets' superiority over conventional police jetcopters will be used to the advantage of crime.' "

"In short," Rourke concluded, "we can nail them there!"

"If we're in time," Manny said glumly.

ROURKE sent his little copter windmilling through the darkness, detouring in a wide circle around the slender, glowing fingers of the commercial towers of Atom Town. Robbie Simakov sat silently beside him, huddled deep in her own thoughts and reflections.

"You're with the World Police then," was all she said.

The black earth rolled past below, with its sprinkled carpet of warm, friendly sparks where homes nestled snugly in the folds of night. Rourke, exhausted, kept his mind on his flying, watching the pattern of beacon lights below, cursing mentally at the aching throb in his skull.

Copters were clustered in the glow of light flooding from the open doors of one of the big hangars as Rourke swept low over the company field. He swung his copter around and came in fast, making a speed landing that sent them rolling up to the other copters. His gaze swept over the crowd as he slipped out of his ship and limped forward. Plant guards were there, also Sky Troopers, and Lieutenant Ybarra was interviewing Skid Halloway in the midst of the crowd. Halloway was stripped to the waist and a Police medico was bandaging a bullet wound in his right shoulder.

Rourke started as a hand grasped his arm, turned, and stared into the grim, hard features of Ralph Henderson McWilliams, "Oh—hi, Mac," he greeted. "When did you get here?"

"Just now," McWilliams growled. "They dragged me outta bed when this shindig blew off. You look kinda beat-up yourself, boy."

"I was at Weigand's," Rourke told him. "They killed him, took the plans to the airocket. What happened here?"

"The girl and Czecmeloweicz dropped in just as Skid was about to take one of the airockets up for a test," Mac explained curtly. "You able to travel, boy?"

Rourke raised his brows. "I got this far!"

"Then come on—I might need you!"

McWilliams pulled him around the crowd and into the lighted hangar. The other two airockets were ignored in the excitement. Mac jerked open the door on one and pushed Rourke through it, following and hustling him on into the cabin high on the broad back of the hull. "Buckle your seat straps," he warned breathlessly. "This is going to be a rough ride!"

Rourke started to protest. "See here, shouldn't Halloway—"

"All that kid knows is how to run a spaceship to the

Moon!" Mac snapped acidly. "I may have a tin leg, but I've forgot more about aerial fighting than this whole bunch put together. Buckle your straps!"

THE CROWD turned startled faces toward the rocket craft as Mac flipped on the power, then scattered wildly as the airocket nosed its way out of the hangar. Mac cut in the ship radio, leaving the videophone screen blank. "Charley X to Control Tower. Request immediate takeoff clearance, Runway Six," he barked.

"Tower to Charley X. Identify yourself, over."

"This is McWilliams! Snap to it, tower—I'm taking off!"

The airocket went hurtling up in a steep climb.

"I'd have taken the old turboprop ship," Mac remarked casually, "only it'd taken too long to fuel her up. I figure they headed straight for Mexico; what do you think?"

"Mexico," Rourke gasped, the acceleration shoving him back into the cushions. Pain lanced through his taped chest.

Mac nodded solemnly and dumped the nose. The airocket leveled off and went into a straining turn, then settled into a headlong flight. "Suppose you get on the videophone now," Mac suggested, "and use some of that smooth salesmanship of yours to get us a UN Armed Forces patrol fighter up here?"

Rourke's eyes widened. "You think we can catch them?"

"I got a hunch I know more about using tailwinds than that crook does." Mac grinned mirthlessly. "We'll catch up with them—then we'll bring that patrol fighter down to clobber them."

Rourke got onto the videophone, dialing furiously.

Manny's face splashed on the screen. "Tom! Did you get them?"

"Too late," Rourke spoke brusquely. "Manny, get this through Headquarters to the UN Armed Forces Base at San

Antonio. We need a patrol fighter in a hurry—our course is straight south from Atom Town toward Mexico. McWilliams and I are chasing them; we're both in airockets—"

"Have that fighter-pilot contact us!" Mac interjected.

"Got that," Manny acknowledged. "There'll be a fighter up there inside twenty minutes."

CHAPTER FIVE
Fire Control!

"YOU KNOW, I sometimes wonder about you, Rourke," Mac drawled laconically. "Getting a rise out of them yet?"

"They won't answer," Rourke answered in disgust, switching off the videophone.

"Well, if they won't listen, we can't tell them anything—" Mac turned his head and stared out through the transparent blister. His gnarled hands gripped the controls with caressing tenderness akin to pure affection. The airocket swerved gently through the night.

The blue jet-flame of the other airocket was sharply visible against the black earth below. Mac kept one eye on it and the other on the dials and gauges of the chrome-trimmed instrument bank before him. They were boring steadily into the darkness with only a faint hissing sound of jets from the rear of the ship and a gentle, wallowing motion when it cut through some atmospheric turbulence. Rourke tried the videophone again.

"World Police to Lipenchek in experimental airocket! Come in if you hear me, Lipenchek. We have a patrol fighter on the way. You haven't a chance unless you surrender. Come in, Lipenchek—"

There was no response.

"Least they aren't taking any evasive action," Mac commented. "That guy's just high-tailing it as fast as he can go. Probably never got his feet off the ground until they stopped making automobiles." The Old Man sighed and poked a cigarette between his lips. "This is the way it always ends up, isn't it. Whether they're fancy-pants dictators with a nation of fanatics to do their dirty work, or just plain filthy crooks with the law on their trail—"

"Yeah," Rourke said. He stared bitterly at the blank videophone screen. "This is how it ends up. Got a cigarette?"

Mac passed him the pack and lighter. "Seems funny the way dictators have gone out of style—even in the small countries—"

"World opinion," Rourke replied, lighting himself a smoke. "Dictators are no longer respected, that's all. It's like the savage tribes that once were cannibals." He returned the pack and lighter and slumped back in his seat. "Those savages gave up cannibalism when they got in contact with the outside world and learned what scorn and disgust their customs won in others' eyes. Same way with dictators."

"So now we've got world criminals. It hasn't changed much!"

"Fewer innocent people are killed, is all," Rourke agreed absently. "It takes all types to make a world—but the killers we have to eliminate…"

MAC STARED out at the other ship, saw it change course slightly, and moved the controls to follow it. "They're ducking for the mountains." He blew smoke and grinned at Rourke. "I used to make practice radar runs over this country—know every rock and gully."

"Where's our patrol fighter?" Rourke wondered.

"He'll be along. What do you think of the increase in world population, though? We stopped wars and we control famine—"

"If we control birth rate, now, we'll have it perfect!" Rourke smiled; he was beginning to like old man McWilliams. "Or do you prefer wars and famine?" he asked mockingly.

"Nuts to both!" Mac retorted. "And nuts to your compulsory birth control, too. Preach me no Utopias, sonny—I've heard that tune before! The world's getting overpopulated; there's only one answer to any man worth his salt." He hooked a gnarled thumb toward the glittering stars. "Out there! We'll have to start colonizing Mars before too long."

"Still, birth control wouldn't hurt," Rourke needled him, mirthfully. "It simply wasn't handled right. A bunch of government 'experts' tried to cram it down peoples' throats! It's no wonder public opinion rebelled—"

Mac was giving a derisive snort when the call-light blinked green. He reached over and flipped the radio switch.

"UNAF Official Six-Four to Inspector Thomas Rourke. Acknowledge, please. Over."

Rourke leaned forward to reply, but Mac grasped his arm. "You're the brass here," he said quickly, "but put this fighter-jockey on my orders—I can run this mission!"

Rourke nodded, then spoke to the blank screen. "Inspector Rourke to UNAF Official Six-Four. Acknowledged; give your position. Over."

"Six-Four to Rourke. Am cruising at forty thousand; have you and the target both on my radarscope, directly below. With your permission, Inspector, I'll discharge a missile to finish the target and go home." The pilot's tones were flippant. *"Is that okay? Over."*

Mac was shaking his head emphatically. Rourke winked at him and spoke to the screen. "Six-four, that is not okay. Repeat, that is not okay. You will stand by and accept orders from my pilot, McWilliams. Acknowledge. Over."

"Six-four to Rourke. I'm to take orders from McWilliams. Over." The pilot sounded disgruntled.

Mac grabbed the screen and pivoted it to his side. "This is McWilliams—Mac to you, sonny. Open channel on this. I know you're logged with enough napalm, robot missiles, bombs, and guns to rip up a good-sized fortress by the roots, but this target is touchy—got that?"

"Open channel. Got it."

"Good, good. I'll give you fire control visual, but first here's the brief: our target is an experimental airocket, manned by criminals. They have important aircraft plans with them that must not be destroyed. You'll have to set up your nose-cannon for a direct-fire pass—"

"But you're dodging through hills down there! I'd pile up at my speed!"

"There's some wide valleys in here too," Mac consoled him with a grin. "I'll have to call you down when you can dip into one and hit our target on the button. It's a setup for an angular attack; gauge about a one-second burst—"

"What d'you know about armament?"

"Son, I jockeyed jets before your daddy's voice changed. Stand by now—we're due to be crossing a valley in about three minutes now—"

"Wilco!" There was a surprised respect in the pilot's voice.

Mac switched the cabin lights off.

AS ROURKE'S eyes adjusted to the darkness he began to make out the black humps of mountains below them. Slightly ahead now was the other ship's blue jet-fire. He could make out the sleek outline of its hull in the dim starlight, the glint of the transparent blister over its cabin.

"Three hundred miles an hour," Mac stated brusquely. "I've got to admit that guy knows the mountain peaks around here—or else he's a fool! Six-four, I'm moving in on him—"

"Don't risk their fire!"

"With hand guns? They stick a gun out at this speed, the wind'll tear their hand off!" Mac hunched over the controls, peering ahead. "Steady, six-four. Forty thousand. Southeast, four miles. Set your guns—

"Now!"

The two airockets shot between looming, black peaks and hissed out over a broad, starlit valley.

It came and went in the blink of an eyelash. Out of the starry heavens, a shimmering, wicked-looking steel insect, its fins bristling with armament. Curving down into the valley, swooping straight toward the chubby airocket ahead. Orange flame blossomed from its needle-nose. Then it curved up, dwindling back into the night, leaving a blue streak of jet-fire behind it.

The airocket ahead jolted with the impact of 70-mm cannon shells. Pieces of its hull flew away and a misty cloud of gasses enveloped it. The inertium bladder was punctured, the gasses escaping, condensing in the outer air—

Then it was plunging downward to the boulder-strewn floor of the valley. It struck with an erupting cloud of sand and rock.

"Mission accomplished," Mac drawled. "You can go home now, six-four."

"Glad to oblige, old timer! Sixty-four over and out."

MAC PEELED the airocket through a turn that skirted the steep face of a cliff, then brought it around toward the, dark, broken hulk of the wreck below. He flared out, dropped the wheels, and eased the ship onto a wide strip of level, sandy wash.

"Flashlights in the tool compartment," he said. Rourke unstrapped and climbed back to get them.

They dropped down to the rocky ground and picked their way over it toward the wreck. Rourke shivered in the crisp, predawn chill. Mac paused and swept the beam of his flashlight over the torn, twisted hull. "Nothing alive in that," he said dryly.

"It's a wonder the heat from the rocket unit didn't set the ship afire," Rourke mused.

"The rocket cut off automatically," Mac explained, then shrugged. "Well, let's get it over with."

The forward section of the hull was completely smashed, telescoped and shoved back into the midsection. The sealite gas-bladder hung out of a gaping rent in the side like a sick tongue. They walked up to the front of the wreck and lifted off the shattered remains of the cabin blister.

The body of Jan Lipenchek, alias Czecmeloweicz, was a flabby rag doll thrown amidst the litter of the cabin floor. Miss Dorothea "Trixie" Finch had her lovely shape imbedded firmly in the instrument panel. Rourke stared down at the twisted head, the smear that had been a beautiful, appealing face.

She wasn't whistling now.

"NEW YORK'S on the line, darling!"

Rourke muttered a curse, tore a sheet of paper out of the typewriter and crumpled it into a ball, flinging it to the floor. He whirled in his swivel chair, reaching across the desk to flip the switch from *intercom* to *videophone.*

Bill Warner's fleshy features stared back at him from the screen. "Hello, Tom."

"Hi," Rourke said, scowling.

"How's that article coming?"

"I'm writing it, man. I'm writing it."

Warner recoiled slightly. "Oh. Having trouble?"

"Oh no—nothing at all! I haven't had a thing to think about for weeks but your little old article—"

"Take it easy," Warner protested. "It's enough to have my boss jumping me because your article's not in, without you giving me a hard time! When'll you have it?"

"In the morning." Rourke slumped back, disgusted.

"Tonight," Warner insisted. "Get it on the midnight strato-express. My chair's getting hot."

"Say listen—I'm a big wheel now—a hero!" Rourke made wild gestures at the screen. "Tell your boss how lucky he'll be to get an article with my byline!" He grabbed a newspaper off the stack on his desk and shoved it before the screen. "Look!"

Warner looked. Big headlines read: AIROCKETS EXEC HELPS POLICE CRACK WORLD CRIME RING.

"I know" Warner said. "That's the point."

"What's the point?"

"The boss wants your article," Warner explained. "Now, chum. While you *are* a hero. The Martian Expedition returns next month."

"Oh." Rourke slumped again, crestfallen. "I thought—well, never mind."

Warner grinned slyly. "Tonight then?"

"Okay!" Rourke waved feebly at the screen. "I'll send it off tonight. Give my love to all the little bug-eyed monsters."

"Right!" Warner chuckled warmly. "So long—*hero*..."

Rourke looked up in time to see a slim, shapely arm push open the office door. "Go right in, sir!" a soft voice spoke bewitchingly.

"*Ahem*—thank you!" Manny strode through the door, his brows raised and a happy expression on his puggish features. "Hi, Tommy! We got it boy; we got it!" He threw himself into a chair.

"We got what?" Rourke asked suspiciously. "And what's this 'Tommy' routine?"

"Simply that you've got the softest job an Inspector ever had," Manny replied calmly.

"An insp—" Rourke broke off, staring at him. "You mean—I'm still in?"

MANNY nodded solemnly. "It is the considered opinion of Headquarters Staff that you're too valuable a man to be mustered out simply because of the undue publicity you've attracted to yourself in this case. While not only the identity, but the very activities, of a World Police Inspector must normally be kept secret—"

"But—but what about my job here?" Rourke stammered. "What about AiRockets? What about Old Man McWilliams?"

"—However, in your present capacity," Manny went on, unperturbed, "Headquarters finds that you are in a position to be of inestimable service to the United Nations."

"In my—my present capacity?"

"It seems there's a motion before the General Assembly at the moment which calls for the international registration and licensing of all private and commercial airockets—with an international bureau, you understand; not with national bureaus, as with jetcopters. And we're going to need someone on that bureau to see that no sharp politicians pull a loophole deal so a crime syndicate can acquire airockets for its dirty work. AiRockets will be asked to send a representative of the industry, of course—"

"So I'll have both jobs."

Manny's eyes narrowed craftily. "I think Shadow Nine can manage it," he said in a low murmur.

"Are you my contact?" Rourke gave in quietly.

"You're still in my sector." Manny rose from his chair and plodded to the door. "Call me if you need any packages delivered. You know the number—United Air Delivery Service."

Rourke nodded. "Don't ask the brain any embarrassing questions!"

Manny waved a stubby hand, started through the door—and recoiled with an exclamation of pleasure. He grinned and winked at Rourke, then sidled out the side of the door as the smooth, curvaceous young woman passed him on the way in.

"What's been going on in here?" Robbie Simakov demanded with an imperious tilt of her chin.

"I'm writing an article," Rourke said wearily.

"And inspiration just won't come, is that it?" She moved toward the desk, hips swaying to the rhythm of her stride.

"Something like that," Rourke hazarded.

"Well, we shouldn't let these weird-looking little men in to bother snookums then, should we?" She came around the desk. "We should comfort Tommy and—and give him inspiration—"

"Indeed we should!" Rourke agreed.

He wondered, happily, if Warner would mind—*really* mind—if the article didn't get finished until tomorrow...

THE END

FLYING SAUCERS FROM EARTH...OR SOMEWHERE ELSE?

At first it seemed like a weird industrial accident when the welder burned his hand off without uttering the slightest whimper of pain. Then someone took a shot at one of Project Star's leading scientists. Soon the men at the project discovered that the flying disks that they were secretly manufacturing for the government weren't exactly as they were first planned. But who was making these changes—and for what purpose?

What lay ahead for Earth was a nightmare of carnage beyond human comprehension.

CAST OF CHARACTERS

ALAN RACKHAM
He was a top scientist working on a secret project for the government. He soon wondered who he was really working for.

BRAVE
This impressive Navajo had a Herculean build and a granite-like face, but he spoke with the fluency of an Ivy League graduate.

WIN GILMORE
She was a good-looking gal and Alan's fiancée. Yet, there was something about her that seemed different from most people.

JIM McELDOWNIE
On the surface he seemed like a wacked-out sensationalist TV interviewer—but what was the real purpose of his show?

DON MARINER
He was the first to discover that someone or some "thing" had been altering secret government spacecraft designs.

ROB POPE
A longtime employee at Project Star. His job was as a chemist, but his knowledge of hypnotism soon became invaluable.

THE ALIEN LEADER
It was his job to explain to the men of Project Star just exactly why millions of Earthmen had to die!

ARMAGEDDON EARTH

(originally "Armageddon 1970")

By
GEOFF ST. REYNARD

ARMCHAIR FICTION & MUSIC
PO Box 4369, Medford, Oregon   97501-0168

*The original text of this novel was first
published by Greenleaf Publishing Company*

Armchair Edition, Copyright 2011, by Gregory J.   Luce
All Rights Reserved

*For more information about Armchair Books and products, visit our
website at…*

www.armchairfiction.com

Or email us at…

armchairfiction@yahoo.com

CHAPTER ONE

THEY tried to kill Alan Rackham about an hour after he had seen the accident. They bungled the job. They shot at him from ambush—with an ordinary automatic pistol—as he was walking up to his house; and Brave, who had a sixth sense for danger that never failed him, knocked Alan over at the very instant of the shot and sprawled across him, a great solid shield holding him down and protecting him despite his angry wrigglings. Brave's grenade pistol was in his hand before the two of them hit ground, and he sent four quick shots at the bushes, spaced so that the tiny hot fragments tore hell out of thirty yards of shrubbery. Nobody yelled or groaned. Brave waited a full minute, and then he rose cautiously, so that Alan could sit up and brush himself off and swear as he spat out dirt. They went into the house and Alan reported the assassination attempt to his immediate superior, Dr. Getty. After that they didn't try again to kill Alan for a long time.

The accident had been uncanny. It happened in the room where the shells of the silver-colored disks were fitted together and welded, before they were sent to the gargantuan baths that half-melted them again to rechill them into solid masses of metal that nothing short of a direct hit by a blockbuster would crack.

A welder, using one of the newly developed torches that made the old ones seem like match-flares by comparison, dropped it accidentally. Its flame licked up and sprayed across the man's right hand. It melted the protective glove like ice cream on a stove; crisped away the skin and liquefied the flesh, charred the bones black and left the welder no more than half a palm and two fingers before he could jerk his hand out of the terrible blast of fire.

Alan and Brave were standing about twelve feet off, and there could be no mistake as to what they saw then.

THE welder turned off his torch with his left hand; he held the remains of his right hand before his face, turned it and stared at it (the blood coursing in little sluggish streams down the forearm, the charcoal that had been bone sifting off into the air, the flesh a greasy yellow-red mass like candle drippings), and he shook his head slowly, an expression of annoyed mortification on his face. It was as though he had cut himself while shaving, no more. He was simply piqued, when he should have been shrieking with horror and unendurable pain.

Alan and Brave ran to him. "My God, man," said Alan, shaken, "let me get you to infirmary."

The welder stood up. "That's all right, Dr. Rackham. I can go myself. This don't hurt." And then a curious look spread over his face, as if he had just recollected a lesson taught him long ago. "It don't hurt much," he amended. "I guess it's cauterized so bad I can't feel it yet. Don't you worry, sir, I can make it."

He walked away, perfectly steady, carrying the almost destroyed hand in front of his chest; and Alan was so dumbfounded he let him go.

The welder never reached the infirmary. No man saw him again, alive or dead.

So an hour thereafter someone took a shot at Alan Rackham. Since Brave had witnessed the accident too, and because neither of them could account for the shooting except in connection with that strange accident, it seemed stupid and pointless for an attempt to be made on Alan's life alone; especially when a grenade pistol—one of those lean evil handguns developed in 1959—would with one shot have cut an eight-yard-wide swath in everything before it and eliminated both of them. But there it was. They shot at Alan with an automatic—the bullet nicked across his chest and spoiled a blue coat that was practically new—and then they disappeared.

Alan's house, which he shared with Brave, was a four-room brick atop a knoll on the outskirts of the colony. It was a perfect bachelor establishment; the precipitron kept it free of dust and Brave's innate neatness overcame Alan's careless disregard of surroundings to the extent that dirty socks and unpressed trousers were not often to be met with lying in corners or hanging over the backs of chairs. Brave was a good everyday cook and Alan occasionally took a couple of hours off to chef up a New Orleans style banquet for two. The living room was lined with books and the plastiglassed-in lounging quarters in the rear held racks of pipes and a well-stocked bar. They were very comfortable there. It was only a ten-minute walk from Alan's laboratory, and four minutes' ride from the center of the colony.

The colony was called Project Star. It was located on Long Island, protected much as Oak Ridge had been in the '40s and '50s, and Project Bellona in the early '60s; with electrified fences, and soldiers carrying the latest weapons, and a ring of grotesque machinery all around it, comprised of radar detectors and great ack-ack guns and a number of generators that threw up a kind of primitive, partly-effective force field. The force field would stop any aircraft or at least cause it enough trouble to slow it down for the ack-ack.

Of course the artificial satellite, Albertus (named in honor of Albert Einstein), kept a watchful telescope on Project Star. But in that year of 1970 it seemed to most men that all the caution and secrecy was overly dramatic. After the collapse of Russia a decade before from internal causes precipitated by the successful fixing of the American-controlled satellite Albertus in the heavens, and after the almost Carthaginian peace imposed on Argentina when its dictator A-bombed London, the world had quieted down considerably. America was top dog in the nations and her supervision of the science of other countries left little possibility of successful attack or even of effective sabotage within the many colonies that worked on advancements in weapons and other civilized phenomena, and on space flight.

NEARLY everyone believed that the purpose of Project Star was to construct "flying saucers" (the inadequate name had stuck through the years) for use in reaching out to the other planets. Only the men who were working there, and a few others in government and in the military forces, knew that the disks were not intended for extra-terrestrial flight— there were rocket projects galore for that—but for journeys in the atmosphere or slightly above it, at speeds incredible even in 1970. The name Project Star had not been chosen to mislead anyone, but it had done so and nobody bothered to correct the impression. Secrecy had become an ingrained national habit in the past all the way back to World War Two.

Dr. Alan Rackham was one of the scientists who worked on the problem of fuel for the disks. He was not a member of the vastly important handful who headed the colony and came equipped with everything sacred and untouchable except halos, but he was considered of enough consequence to rate a house of his own and an assistant who was also an efficient bodyguard. This was Brave, whose proper name was John Kiwanawatiwa.

Brave sat down in his own chair, a sturdy specially built job, while Alan called Dr. Getty on the visiphone to report the shooting. Brave never sprawled out or slouched as his superior did. He sat straight, a red-copper-colored man built to the scale of a Greek statue, about half again life size. His arms and legs were tough as cable steel, his chest a brawny barrel. He was a Navajo Indian, but his features were more nearly those of a Sioux: a great finely-formed crag of a nose, thin straight lips over white teeth, dark eyes that a hawk might envy their piercing power, a wolf-trap jaw. His speech was that of an M.S. of Carlisle and Oxford, except when he spoke with people he did not know or like; then it became a parody of the nineteenth century storybook red man's gutteral discourse. At times, when he went with Alan to meetings of the hierarchy (a few of whom, including Dr. Getty, he cordially detested for their bland self importance), he even wore a bedraggled chicken feather sticking upright in his black hair, stood behind Alan with folded arms and a fierce expression and confined his remarks to "Ugh" and "Waugh." This gave both Alan and himself a great deal of innocent pleasure.

For Alan Rackham was also a rebel against stuffiness and conceit. He was a perfectly normal-looking man, of slightly more than middle height, thirty-one years old, handsome enough if you liked lean bony features and unruly brown hair; his muscular development was so unobtrusive that no one ever guessed he had been a Marine and won himself a DSC in Argentina. He enjoyed his work at Project Star, for he had a scientist's inquiring mind; but he liked even more the huge Indian with whom he lived, the girl in the metallurgy section who wore his engagement ring, and the book of rather impudent philosophy on which he worked during his free evenings.

He also loved a long drink, a thoughtful pipe, an involved practical joke, and the moody Siamese cat, Unquote.

NOW he turned from the visiphone, as the image of Dr. Getty faded out on its screen, and he frowned at Brave.

"Son," he said, "why would anybody take a potshot at me?"

"What does Doc Pomposity say about it?" rumbled the Indian.

"Mainly blah, blah, blah."

"Naturally," nodded Brave. "You know, sagamore, I think it's that accident. There was something cockeyed about it...I don't care how shocked the fellow was, or how quickly the flame seared up and anesthetized the wound; there should have been plenty of pain in that hand. And he didn't even yip when it happened. He only looked peeved."

"Getty says he never got to the infirmary. No one has seen him at all."

"Cockeyed," said Brave again. "The whole thing's a muddle." He stared at Alan. "Boss, I have an instinct that warns me we're in for trouble."

"That's an instinct? When I get shot at, this gives you an instinct?"

"The noble red man has an instinct," said Brave imperturbably, "which sits in his belly and beats on a tom-tom when trouble's coming. I don't mean ghastly wounds that don't make men cry out, or even lunatics laying for you thereafter—and there's a connection between the two, that's sure. But I mean big trouble. There's something in the air. I can't quite catch it, but it's been there for a long time. Weeks and months, sirdar."

"You've been reading the thesaurus again. You know more synonyms for 'master' than Roget. You mean this seriously, Brave? About trouble?" He had a respect for the Indian's intuition which was based half on his anthropological knowledge of the weird powers of certain older races, and half on pure human superstition; at times when Brave made his predictions, Alan felt as though a gypsy crone had passed by him and whispered some incantation in his ear.

"I mean it, Alan. And the damned instinct has never been

wrong yet. It's beating in my guts right now like it did at Campana just before hell broke loose."

"Well, batten down the hatches, then," said Alan resignedly, while the hair on the back of his neck prickled and tried to stand up. "Your 'trouble' has got itself off to a fine start. My tailor will never be able to mend this jacket."

"Why don't you cook us some Oysters Rockefeller and lobster thermidor and all that Frenchified goop you brew up?" suggested Brave. "If we're in for afflictions, we may as well meet 'em with pleasantly full stomachs."

"Right. While I'm at it, you write a report of the incident—of both of them—and sign my name. Getty'll never know the difference. He thinks you haven't mastered basic English yet."

"Ugh," said Brave. "Noble red man will inscribe little pictures on birchbark for medicine man, while medicine man raises cain in frozen food locker. Don't get that sauce too thin this time, patriarch. I can't bear watery sauce on my lobsters."

CHAPTER TWO

NEXT morning, while Alan was still dressing and yawning, and Brave was clattering skillets in the kitchen, humming the *allegro con passionate* movement from "Hard Hearted Hannah the Vamp of Savannah," the door chimes bonged softly. Brave went to the spywindow, surveyed the caller, and shifted his grenade pistol to a handier position before opening the door. A stranger stood on the threshold.

Ichabod Crane Brave thought to himself, but aloud he said, "Yes?"

"Ah," said the stranger, "you would be the tough egg with

the unpronounceable name. Greetings, chieftain."

"How," said Brave with a straight face. "You want-um audience with great sachem?"

"That I do, Lo."

"Oh, gad," groaned the Indian, "if I hear that weary old jest once more I'll burst into tears and die. Come in, comedian. Dr. Rackham's dressing."

"Thanks. Forgive me for the gosh awful gag, friend. I haven't eaten breakfast yet and an empty stomach plays the devil with my sense of humor." He rattled over to a chair and sat down. At least, thought Brave, closing the door, you expected him to rattle. He was the longest and thinnest bag of bones ever seen on Long Island. Fully six feet eight, he was lean from the top of his narrow skull, which was covered by an inch-long mat of straight stiff blond hair, to the soles of his number twelve feet. If he had any fat in him at all it must have been a very lonesome blob of fat indeed, well camouflaged and utterly alone in a wilderness of stringy muscle, meager sinew, and shaving-slender bones. His green eyes, perpetually half-lidded on either side of a nose like the prow of a Chinese junk, were humorous and sharp and as bright as polished emeralds.

Brave said to himself, *Here is a shrewd customer, who isn't one-tenth the fool he appears to be.*

"You don't have an appointment with Dr. Rackham."

"No, I don't. A plump little meathead called Getty over at the central offices said he'd be here, and I popped over on the chance. I want to entice him onto a TV program of mine."

"Dr. Rackham is a busy man."

"So is President Blose of the U.S. of A., but *he* came on the program, Lo. Pardon me," said the man, "there I go again. It's second nature. I don't mean to offend, but I was a disk jockey once. Look, friend, my name is Jim McEldownie.

I'm *Worlds of Portent* McEldownie."

"I'm *Lashings of Victuals* Kiwanawatiwa, and my eggs are scorching," said Brave, going out to the kitchen. "The books are counted, so are the pipes, and the first editions are booby-trapped. Don't get any ideas."

"My Indian friend, I could grow to love you," said McEldownie. "Seriously though, don't you ever watch TV?"

"I do not."

"That explains it. Existing in the dark like this, you wouldn't have heard of me. I run this show called *Worlds of Portent,* onto which I entice various important and pseudo-important characters, and there I cajole and browbeat and query them until they tell me all sorts of fascinating lies, and the public laps it up like a bunch of silly cats."

UNQUOTE, the Siamese, rose out of her hygienic playbox and gave him a frozen glare. He recoiled. "My God," he said, "I seem to be offending everyone this morning. Forgive me, puss."

Unquote snarled and collapsed in a boneless pile of beautiful fur. Alan stuck his head into the room and said, "Where do you classify me?"

"Huh? Oh, hello, Doc. You're important. Anybody from Project Star is important. Whether the same can be said for those officials of our mighty government who have gasped and babbled and turned blue on *Portent,* I'm not one to declare. How about it, Doc? Will you appear?"

"Talking about what? Fuel? That's all I really know."

"If you can talk for thirteen minutes about it, without violating any regulations or giving away secrets, I want you. Fuel is hot stuff with the space-minded public."

"What do you think, Brave...should we do it?"

Brave said, "Too much time and no fun, that's how it all sounds to me."

"Oh, I don't know. I've never been on the air."

"Please," said McEldownie, shuddering like a leafless willow in a high wind. "The phrase is 'on the space.' Air belongs to that outmoded, decadent, but apparently deathless medium called radio. There, I've said it. Have you got any mouth-washing soap?"

"He's a positive Hilton Boil," said Brave from the kitchen. "A real yukked-up comic. Wait 'til I've fed him and we'll hurl him out."

"All right," said Alan, "I'll do it—might be fun. I'm a ham at heart anyway. When do you want me?"

"Tomorrow night at eight vacant?"

"As vacant as—" he was going to say "Dr. Getty's head," but caught himself in time. The TV man's flippancy was contagious. "Quite vacant. Give Brave the directions and we'll be there."

Brave said, "Breakfast is on. There are three plates and food for two. I hope you eat lightly, Mr. Portent."

"McEldownie, but call me Jim. I eat like a bird."

The bird, thought Alan half an hour later, must be a starving turkey buzzard. Alan sighed and stood up. "We're due at work, Jim. See you at eight tomorrow, then?"

"Seven-fifteen. I have to brief you. Cheers, gentlemen. Apologize to the cat for me. I insulted it a while back and it's been burning holes in my neck ever since." He started to leave, still with the illusion of rattling bonily. Minutes later, Alan and Brave washed up and strolled down to their laboratory.

Nothing happened that day or the next, save for a thorough search for the missing welder, which turned up no trace of him. At seven-fifteen the two friends walked into the TV studio in Manhattan.

"Hi," said McEldownie, waving a long hand. "Sit down and let's talk about fuel." They did so for several minutes.

At one point the lean man said, "Here's an idea. What if Brave were to stand behind you all through the program? It'd look impressive as hell. Sinister Indian guards scientist even on national hookup. 'No precaution too elaborate for our men,' says head of Project Star. How about it?"

Alan looked at Brave. He would not expose his friend to stupid ridicule. Brave winked. "Okay," said Alan. "But no gags."

"Abso-bloody-lutely. Play it for gravity. Show people that there is danger connected with the business. And I think there is," he added solemnly.

Alan stared. "Why do you say that?"

"I don't mean the TV, I mean your work out on Long Island. You can't tell me that nobody in the world wishes our country any ill will, chum. We have enemies just as we always have had. Why else the ack-ack guns and force screens?"

Alan did not answer. He thought of Brave's prediction of trouble, and he was more impressed with the lanky comedian than he had been before that moment.

THIRTY seconds before the program time he sat down at the round table opposite McEldownie, and Brave took up a forbidding posture behind his chair.

His host began to speak, and suddenly Alan realized why the tall blond irrepressible fellow had been trusted with a program of such gravity as *Worlds of Portent*. As the cameras rolled and the brilliant lights came on, the jester's motley dropped away from him and was replaced by a cloak of earnest sobriety. His fantastic appearance heightened the seriousness; it was as shocking and thought-producing as if a scarecrow had begun to talk Schopenhauer.

He knew precisely how much to say; when to sit back and let Alan do a monologue, and when to interrupt with a pertinent question. He was a genius at his work.

And then, perhaps four or five minutes after the telecast had begun, Alan became aware of two things, each quite extraordinary. First, Brave had disappeared. Alan glanced back over his shoulder and found the Indian had vanished. The lights were so bright that his vision did net extend to the walls of the studio, so he presumed that his friend was still there somewhere; but he had left the range of the cameras. And secondly, something was happening to Alan's mind.

He tried to analyze the trouble, but he could not do it. He could only touch a few salient points of it. Although he was talking very learnedly and with (so far as be could tell) lucidity and vigor, he was not controlling his tongue in the least. It was almost like being drunk; there seemed to be a small entity perched at the root of his tongue who was pulling the strings of speech. But whereas the tongue of a drunk could be malicious and get himself into all sorts of rows and riots, this particular entity was doing what seemed to be a fine job for him. However, he knew quite well that he himself was not forming or directing the words he spoke. It was unpleasant, to say the least.

And there was something else. His mind, freed of necessity to concentrate on the program, was somewhere off in space, listening intently…listening to a voice from without and within, a voice that inhabited the cold wastes of time and infinity as well as the bone-bounded sphere of his brain.

Listen to me, Alan Rackham, said the voice. Wordlessly, yet with words, from the farthest stretches of the galaxies and still existing in the core of his own intellect, cold as morning frost, hot as insanity's rage, gentle and persuasive as a doting mother, the voice said to him, *Listen to me.*

HE would not listen. It was good and evil both together, and if he listened he would die. Yet it said he would live. He would live forever; if time can be measured in terms of endlessness, he would not die. But he knew he would die. He struggled. The cameras picked up no hint of the travail. His face was intense and good-humored and his words were intelligent; and all the while he fought with the voice and would not listen. He fought it for an hour, and for a month, and until the end of the world came and beyond, and it spoke to him, fire and ice in the same words, but without words, and then he began to listen to it.

At this point six minutes of the telecast had gone by.

You are listening now, said the voice. You are listening, are you not?

I'm listening. God curse you.

I am taking you, Alan Rackham, as a bear takes a lamb, as a man takes a woman, as a hand takes a glove and the glove takes the hand.

I understand, curse you. Take me.

I am older than your whole race, and wiser than its cumulative wisdom, and I come from the stars.

Of course, you come from the stars. You are myself, and I understand you, friend.

Yes, I am yourself, wiser and stronger and older and beyond you in every way, and I am you. You are my servant, my slave, and myself.

Certainly, master. Why do you tell me things I have always known?

You are not obeying when you follow me, for you follow yourself, you who are now me.

You are God, are you not? said Alan in his mind. *The Buddhists are right.*

No. Not God. I am the atom and I am the intergalactic void, you and I and everything right and wrong. Have you learned your lesson?

It is a lesson I knew in the womb.

Now you are mine, said the voice, approving without an iota's loss of the flame and frost of hatred and love blended flawlessly.

This is a pleasure beyond pleasure, sensation far above sensation. This is maelstrom descent and flying into the sun. This is the keenness of sexual transport to the nth power. I live for you.

Now you have it. Never forget it.

Never! swore Alan.

Now forget it.

I have forgotten it.

Now what do you have to do for me?

Whatever it is you wish.

Truly you are mine. Now you have forgotten me.

I have forgotten.

Who am I?

Who are you? asked Alan, perplexed.

Truly you have forgotten. What have you to say?

"So the problem of most importance confronting us then was, how can we carry enough of this fuel to get us to the moon and back? It took us years to solve that one, but as everyone knows, we did. Then Van Horne discovered the hitherto unknown properties of—" he was talking blithely, almost by rote, for this was history book stuff, and there had never been any entity guiding his tongue at all, nor any voiceless voice in the bitterness of the eternal chasm between the stars and there was no memory anywhere in his consciousness of such things, nor any lingering uncomfortable feeling that he had known a thing now forgotten...

CHAPTER THREE

THEY were driving out Queens Boulevard toward the colony, and Alan said, "Why did you leave, Brave? Where'd you go?"

The great Indian spun the wheel for a curve. "Just back to the wall."

"Why?"

"Lights were too bright for my eyes."

Alan stared at him. "You could out-gaze the sun, you pokerfaced liar, and you know it. Why did you leave?"

Brave glanced over at him. "I hate to go on sounding like a spae-wife, or the Witch of Endor. But never in all my life have I had such a succession of ominous bodings. You'll think I'm turning raven in my old age—"

"No, damn it, Brave, I know you can smell danger a mile or a month away. Go ahead."

"Quoth the raven, then. I didn't feel happy about standing there. Before we started, it seemed like a good quiet joke. But when we were there and the lights came on, and the cameras started, I suddenly had to step back out of sight. I *had* to, Alan. A couple of my ghostly ancestors took me by the scruff and hauled me right away from there."

"That would have made a nice tableau on TV."

Brave chuckled deep in his chest. "Running Lizard and Pony Sees-the-Sky saving John Kiwanawatiwa from the white man's magic...I laugh, viceroy, but I swear it felt like that. The old desert-spawned blood—the blood that doesn't tame down—boiled up under those lights and cameras. It pulled the civilized flesh and bones away from them. It whispered that things were wrong, wrong for an Indian and wrong for his friend." He stepped on the gas viciously and the MG spurted forward onto the Union Turnpike like a racing hound. "Alan, I almost yanked you up and walked off with you under my arm. I didn't like you sitting there in the bath of electrical magic."

"Why didn't you do it?" asked Alan curiously.

"Oh, hell, boss man. It's one thing to have these primeval urges, and another to forget all your technical training and scientific knowledge so completely that you'll follow the impulse. Do you bust a window every time you'd like to?"

"Hmm." Alan was ill at ease. It seemed to him for a

moment that there was something to Brave's instinct, and that he should have been snatched from those lights. Then he said, "I think it's merely that someone had a shot at me the other day, and you've fretted over that till you're seeing assassins behind every chair."

"Maybe. Maybe." Brave rocketed the little car along the dark highway, across the miles to home, and all the while the tom-toms beat in his blood and he knew that he should be afraid, that he should be coldly and sanely afraid of some black hazard soon to come.

DON Mariner walked into their laboratory the following afternoon. He was one of the top engineers on Project Star, a youngish-middle-aged man turning to flab and ever-thinning hair. Ordinarily good-humored, today he had a long face and a crease between his eyes. Without a word he spread a sheaf of blueprints and photostats out on a lab table. Alan and Brave bent over them. Don's stubby finger traced the outline of a flying disk, then stabbed at the fuel storage tanks and several other sections of the interior.

"Look at this, you two. I've had it under my nose for three months and it never struck me till today. Just look at it. See anything wrong?"

After a moment Alan said, "The fuel tanks are too big."

"You ought to be the engineer instead of me. I ought to hire out as a potato peeler. Three months it took me to see it."

"What's the point of it?" asked Brave. "If the disks are going to use hornethylene, they won't need a tenth—not a hundredth that much storage space, even if they want to circle the earth a dozen times without landing."

"Here's another thing," said Don Mariner. "This closet for space suits. Why? The stratosphere is the highest they're supposed to go, and there's no need for space suits there.

You'd want a space suit to crawl around the outside of Albertus, but not to wear in a disk. If there's trouble outside the shell you will simply land. Now look at these instruments." He showed them another chart. "Are these instruments for earth travel?"

"I don't know. Are they?"

"They are not. And also they're not the instruments Carey designed for the disks last year. They're a new set entirely, and some of them I don't understand myself, but I'll tell you this…they're not for earth travel. They're what you'd want in a space rocket." He looked up, his gray eyes bleak. "I faced Carey with these, and he swears they're his old design—and Carey doesn't lie in the ordinary course of events. But they're not, and I know it."

"What's the point?" asked Alan. The question was almost rhetorical—he knew the answer.

"The point is, these disks we're building are supposed to be purely and simply a faster means of traveling around Terra than any we have now. But the man in the street, that faceless brainless little cipher, believes they're for conquering the stars. And by Judas, he's right! We're building interplanetary disks—*and we're not supposed to know it.*"

The three men stared at one another.

"Who's keeping it from us?" asked Mariner.

"And why?" added Alan.

"There are plenty of rocket projects—so what if someone wants to try a space disk instead? Why would he tell all his scientists and technicians a pack of lies? There's no need for secrecy, for God's sake!"

"But—my gosh," protested Alan, "no one man could keep a thing like this from all the rest of us. There must be ten or twenty who know. And details like these, the fuel tanks and instruments, they can't be hidden from anybody."

"So where does it lead us?"

"Up a narrow, dank, ill-smelling blind alley," said Brave.
"Not so blind—"

THERE was a detonation outside the lab; a harsh,
clangorous thunderclap of a sound, like the bursting of a
bomb full of wash tubs and anchor chains. The three men
were dashing for the door before the reverberations had died
away.

A disk had crashed on the airfield! Brave and Alan and
Don piled into a jeep and raced toward it.

"I didn't know they had any ready for use," Alan shouted.

"Oh, yes. They haven't advertised it much, though. And
this must be the first test flight. I didn't know it was coming
off today."

"You'd think we'd all have been invited to the takeoff.
Big impressive show, faithful workers get afternoon off, and
all that."

"Hell," said Don, "if they're keeping the purpose of the
things from us, for no good reason that I can see, they might
want to keep the test flight secret too."

"How can they keep it secret? It obviously had to take off
in plain sight, and they couldn't shoo everyone indoors. No,
I guess they just didn't give a damn about telling us.
Underlings, unimportant servants—that's us," said Alan
bitterly, with a flash pre-vision of the terrible idea that would
soon be obsessing him.

They pulled up beside the wreckage of the disk. There
was no danger of explosion due to the peculiar properties of
hornethylene. The giant platter, with its raised top like a hot-
dish cover and its bubble of clear crystal beneath, lay
crumpled and bent, one-third of its whole edge accordioned
in upon itself. Even as they approached the crystal bubble
inched open—not smoothly, as it should have done—but like
a damp-swollen door creaks away from its frame under heavy

pressure. The pilot thrust his legs out and dropped to the ground. Alan and a dozen others ran to him.

"Hi," he said. "Guess I messed this job up all right."

"Good Lord, man, are you okay?"

"Not a nick. I just had time to see the ground coming up at me and bingo, I was sitting there with my eyes popping. Anybody got a drink?" He was cut to the pattern of all airmen since the days of monoplanes: tall, narrow of hip and wide of shoulder, lean always-tanned face, a wry grin on the mouth and horizon-hunger in the eyes.

"Were you alone?" asked Alan.

"Sure. They can't risk two guys in these things yet. We don't know what they'll do. This one'll take some going over with a microscope, it's full of bugs. Can someone jockey me over to the main offices?"

The crowd around the disk dispersed slowly. However, Brave put an urgent hand on Alan's arm. It enfolded his biceps and the fingertips met the thumb, for Brave's hands were as outsized as the rest of him. He held Alan there momentarily. "Wait a minute. I want to check something."

"Another instinct, Brave?"

"Plain horse sense. And I want to check it before the big boys clamp a top secret sign on this wreck."

He reached up and gripped the edge of the crystal bubble. It resisted him. He set his muscles and tugged with all his incredible strength. The crushed metal hinges complained and shrieked and parted, and the great bulbous sheet of plasti-quartz fell to the ground, narrowly missing him as he dodged back.

"I'll boost you up, and you can give me a hand."

INSIDE the disk, they crouched and went through the tunnel into the control room. This comprised the entire central portion of the disk. Suspended within the shell, like a small kernel in a large nut, it was held comparatively steady as the outer husk rocked and rolled and flipped in its characteristic skipped-rock flight. Alan did not understand the principle of this near motionless suspension of the control room within an erratically weaving hull, although Don Mariner had tried to explain it to him in patient two-syllable words. It involved a knowledge of the newest developments in gyroscopics, which the young fuel expert did not comprehend. Brave had a fairly good idea of the basic laws involved, but wisely had never tried to beat it into his friend's head. Alan on fuel, on chemistry, on philosophy, was superb. But Alan on dynamics or any other branch of mechanics was deplorable.

They looked around the room. Nearly all the equipment was still in its place, for the clamps that held it during the astonishing speeds the disk could maintain in flight had held it still in the shattering instant of the crash. But the entire control board, the panels of instruments and the wide mirrors that gave the pilot a view of the earth and air from every angle, had all been shoved back and broken when the saucer had struck its nose edge into the ground.

Brave walked over to the pilot's seat and stood silently surveying the mess. At last he said, "Alan."

"Yes?"

"Look here."

Alan looked, and started as though he had been stabbed with a hypodermic needle. "Gawd..." he said.

The control board had buckled back against the pilot's chair; something beyond it, some ponderously heavy piece of machinery in the space between central room and shell, had knifed through wall and board as sharp and deadly as the blade of a guillotine. The metal had sliced the center of the pilot's seat to within six inches of the back.

No man could have sat there at the moment of the crash,

as the pilot asserted he had done.

He would never have lived. He would have been cut in two...

CHAPTER FOUR

THAT night Alan and Brave rode across Project Star to the women's building, where Alan's fiancée, Win Gilmore had a small apartment. Win—short for Winifred, and God help the man who called her *that*—opened the door before the sound of the doorbell had died away.

The first thing that struck one about Win was color—she looked as though she had been put together by a Bergdorf Goodman display artist with a genius for analogous chromas. Her hair was washed in a pale aquamarine and dusted over with luminous flecks of mauve. It was drawn back to the crown and clasped there by an abstract spiral of silver, from which it fell in darkening waves down her naked back. Her nylon jersey lounging outfit, cut with almost severe simplicity, was graduated from pink to a deep violet hue. Her finger and toenails were lacquered with phosphorescent sapphire, and the lashes of her blue eyes were dyed with mascara of the same glowing shade.

Her skin was a soft golden color, thanks to half an hour a day under the sun lamps of the colony's gymnasium.

"How, oh squaw-of-rainbow-brilliance," said Brave, holding up a hand in grave salute. "I leave this warrior in your keeping, whilst I shuffle down to the rec-room and squander a few bucks on the pinball machines."

"How, oh mountain-that-walks. Will you have a slug of Scotch first?"

"The noble red man, pampering his internal workings,

drinks only rum this week. No thanks, Win. The gambling fever's got me. See you."

Alan closed the door behind him and took Win into his arms. He kissed her, gently at first, then hard, their lips parted, warm on each other as their bodies warmed, his hands strong and taut on her back. He smoothed his fingers down the hollow of her spine, ran them up into her soft hair. She said against his mouth, "You demolish that toilsomely-wrought thatch of hair, boy, and I'll demolish you." He laughed and pushed her away and lit a cigarette, stray flecks of mauve from her hair glittering on his fingers.

She went to the low cocktail table and picked up an already filled glass. He took it from her. "Here's atomic dust in your eye, Winifred," he toasted, and drank long and thirstily.

"Whoa, Nellie. Haven't you had anything to drink today?"

"Only the dregs of woe," he said lightly, and then his lean face changed and his eyes looked into a remote place that they did not like. At once she touched his arm.

"Sit down, Alan."

He did so automatically, and she perched tailor-fashion on the edge of the couch beside him. "What's the matter?"

"I wish I knew."

"Just the blues? You been skipping meals? That always makes you ethereal and moody. I'd as soon have Unquote with a toothache around the place as you after you've missed your lunch."

"No, not the blues. Big trouble, sweetheart, that's been exploding right and left with no rhyme nor reason to it. I've thought so much about it in the last few hours that I doubt if I can even talk about it now."

THEN, of course, he told her everything, beginning with the welder's accident and eerie lack of pain; then the shot from the bushes; Brave's indefinite fears climaxing at the telecast; Don Mariner's discovery of the undreamed of potentials of the disks; the crackup ending the almost furtive test flight, and the pilot who lived when he should have been butchered. Alan brought it all out, and as he listened to his own words, a dreadful idea was born and grew and expanded throughout his intellect until suddenly he knew that here was his answer, that no other could be rationally accepted. He sat silently for minutes, while Win watched him, and gradually the color swept out of his face and he began to shiver.

She put the glass into his hand. He drained off the last of the drink, and she clicked open a deep drawer of the cocktail table and gave him another, freshly mixed at a touch of her finger on the emerald stud of the drawer.

"What is it, Alan? You've seen something in it, some connection between these events. What is it?"

He took a shuddering breath through open lips and said, "Yes, I know. I know what we have to fight."

"Fight? You mean there are enemies? You can deduce that from—"

"Yes...there are enemies." He turned, to fix her with a glare like a lunatic's. "Listen, Win. We all have the desire to go out to the other planets, and to the stars beyond our system. We've built a score of rocket projects all over the continent because of that desire. It's no secret, everyone has it. Right?"

"Sure, darling. Even I want to see—well, Mars, anyway."

"But here are these disks, too good, too damned good by far, possibly capable of doing just that; and the government and most of us have thought they were only for earth travel. Why? Who would want to build ships for interplanetary, or even for all I know interstellar-space flight, and keep it hidden from the rest of mankind?"

"Russia?" she suggested humbly.

"Oh, nuts. You might as well say Switzerland. No, it's here at home, on Project Star, and it's a handful or more than a handful of our own top men.

"Now the other angle, there are men here who apparently can't be hurt by ordinary means, who don't feel pain, who can resist the force of such a weapon as a thousand-pound cutlass-edged juggernaut, and who only stare quietly when their hands are melted off like butter in a flame."

"Yes?"

"Put the two together, Win. Remember that after I'd seen one evidence of this lack of pain, I was ambushed. Someone thought I ought to die before I spread the word around. Who?"

"Well, who?"

He drank again and lit a cigarette. The lighter shock in his hand. "There's only one answer I can see," he said. "Correct me if I'm crazy, baby. There are mutants among us. We've been anticipating them in fiction for decades. Now they're here, and they want to reach the stars before we do, they want to pass unnoticed until they're ready to—to take over, or whatever their purpose is."

"Mutants, Alan?"

"The natural progression from Homo Sapiens. Homo superior. The supermen."

SHE slid a pointer across its bar two notches and pressed the emerald button and the table delivered a dry Martini, which she sipped as she regarded him steadily. At last she said, "Is that the sole possibility, sweetheart? Isn't it a pretty wild explanation to accept on the evidence of a couple of queer accidents?"

"I don't think so," he said gruffly. "No, blast it, I don't think it's too wild. It's perfectly possible, and it fits the facts."

"Your Homo superior must be about as fallible as poor old sapiens, then because he's let his secrets out with a vengeance. I'd think that anyone smarter than we are would at least simulate pain after his hand was burned off."

"That was a slipup, yes. But he didn't know anyone was watching."

"Homo superior must have a low opinion of our intelligence, or he wouldn't have let those blueprints get into our hands."

"The progression of the disks' manufacture has come to the point where it couldn't be helped, I suppose. And maybe by now it doesn't matter. Don's had those fuel tank charts for three months, because it was necessary that he work on aspects of construction so close to the tanks that it was impossible to falsify them. But he only saw the instrument panel plans this morning. As I said, maybe it doesn't matter now. If the disks are near enough ready to be taking test flights, maybe the mutants are going to step out in the open."

"Then why would they shoot at you?"

"Hell, I don't know. Perhaps they'll publish the purpose of the disks without mentioning their own roles, as secret designers and builders and as creatures that can't be hurt. They could say 'security reasons' and get away with a lot."

"It's an explanation, all right," said Win. "I don't swallow it, boy, but it does fit the facts. So do all sorts of other weird theories."

"Such as?"

"Ah, you don't want my ideas. They're as mad as your own." She leaned over the arm of the couch and touched several glowing spots on its outer surface; at once the illumination of the room cooled and faded. The forest green walls, complimentary to her own coloring and to the clothing she wore, appeared to recede and become the dark depths of a woodland on a moonless night; the furniture seemed to change into moss-grown stumps and great misshapen rocks. Overhead, the ceiling turned dusky blue under the play of hidden tint-beams, and miniature galaxies twinkled and gleamed across its surface, their varying incandescence giving the illusion of tridimensional infinity.

Alan set down his glass and looked over at her. She was a shape of nocturnal secrecy, sinuous darkness against which her nails and eyelashes burned with phosphorescent sapphire. Her use of the luminous lacquer was an artful bit of technique. It made her into a fantastic mystery that cried out to be solved. Although Alan had seen the trick before, he could never resist it. It was unbelievable that the sober girl in a shapeless smock who sweated in the metallurgy lab was also this Cleopatra, this shadowy temptress. Troy's exquisite Helen, yearning for love, her strong enchantments designed to make her both conqueror and conquest.

FORGETTING the half-smoked cigarette between his fingers, forgetting the supermen and everything else but his physical craving, he threw himself down on the wide couch beside her. His hands touched the live softness of the halter and slid to her back. The sweet strong muscles glided under his fingers as she lifted her arms to take his face between her hands. Then his hands went down from flesh to fabric and he felt her long body pressing tightly against him, close as his own skin.

He opened his eyes and saw the glowing purple of her lashes and in the thick gloom the dimmed luster of her teeth between the parted lips. He kissed her and closed his eyes again. He touched her throat, where the blood throbbed close to the surface in a fast steady rhythm. He found other pulses and held his fingertips on them until his own caught their beat and merged with it and the separate throbbings were one.

It was dark, then very dark, the dark of a sunless sea lapping all about them, and slowly it grew lighter and he was sitting up to run his fingers through his unmanageable hair and remember that some time ago he had been holding a cigarette.

"Hey," he said, "what happened to my cigarette?"

Win stretched out a lazy arm and brought the lights up once more. "Sure you didn't put it out?"

"I swear I didn't. Wait…here it is," he said, picking it off the couch where it had been smashed and its tobacco scattered. "What did I stub that out on?"

"Probably the couch. It doesn't matter, it's resistant."

He looked carefully but could find no place where a cigarette's fire might have been crushed. He shrugged. "So long as I didn't burn you, baby."

"You didn't." She had the automatic table mix them two cocktails. There was a soft knock. "There's Brave back from the rec-room," she said.

"Ears like a fennec," he said admiringly. "I didn't hear anything."

"Watch it, brother. I know what a fennec's ears look like." She went to open the door for the big Indian. "How'd you do, Brave?"

"Gambled away a dollar and seventy-five cents in a reckless passion. Are you ready to go home, sheik?"

"Yes, I am. I have a theory I want to talk about."

"You argue him out of it, Brave," said Win. "He's been working too hard. He thinks supermen are after him."

Brave looked at Alan and his fine face grew hard and set. "Supermen," he said. "Mutants. Alan, is that it?"

"I think that's it."

"It fits the picture, all right."

"It explains every instance we've observed."

"I believe you're on the right track," nodded Brave.

"When did you think of it?"

"While I was talking with Win. Let's go home and thrash it out. She's a disturbing influence.'"

Brave eyed Win up and down with a leer that on anyone else would have been particularly lewd and lascivious. From the faithful Brave it was merely what he meant it to be—a piece of mild buffoonery. "You understate the case, my liege. Yon woman has a plump and supple look; she wriggles too much, such minxes are dangerous. Let's drag tail."

"Okay, boys. Go knock your steel-plated skulls together. But remember that I think you're barking up an impossible tree at an invisible possum what ain't thar." She swung the door open for them and stood aside, one arm upraised with the hand on the jamb.

Alan kissed her a light farewell, and Brave patted her on the head and said, "Ketch-um sleep, squaw, you look bushed." Then, as Alan turned away, his glance was caught by a mark on Win's arm. It was a round blemish, an angry-looking red welt to the edges of which still clung infinitesimal flakes of gray ash smudged into the skin. He turned away and walked down the corridor with Brave at his side, and he thought ferociously of every possibility he could imagine, but his mind always came back to the same answer.

It was a burn, just such a small wound as would result, say, from a cigarette being pressed out against the arm by an oblivious lover.

And it should have been shockingly painful.

But Win had not felt it at all…

CHAPTER FIVE

ALAN awoke after an hour of nightmare-ridden sleep. He opened his eyes and got quietly out of bed and put on his tweed suit and a pair of loafers, then he walked out of the house without disturbing the slumber of Brave.

He went down to the main road and walked along it in the moonlight toward a distant group of buildings. Presently a soldier stepped into his path.

"Halt and identify yourself."

"I am Dr. Alan Rackham of Fuel Research. My security number is $A_{10}C_{14}B_{44}$."

The soldier looked at him a moment and then his eyes glittered. "Pass, friend," he said, and standing aside he watched Alan go on toward the buildings. There was a cynical smile on the soldier's mouth.

Alan came to a squat flat roofed structure like a concrete shed. He knocked on the door. It opened and he went in. One weak bulb burned in a lamp. There was a tall man standing there in the shadows. He shook hands with Alan.

"Welcome, companion. Just sit down here."

Alan seated himself on a stool. The other passed along two walls and in succession a number of vivid lights flared on, bathing Alan in their burning radiance. He did not blink, but looked steadily and fixedly ahead.

Greetings, said the voice.

Greetings, master.

Are you happy to return to me?

I have never been away from you.

That is true. Now I have things to tell you. You will not remember them consciously tomorrow, but you will obey the commands and refuse to do those things that I tell you are wrong. Understood?

Understood.

Now first, slave, said the voice coldly, anger piled on icy anger in the dripping wordless thoughts: *you have decided that there are aliens among you. A race of supermen, mutated from your own weak breed.*

Yes.

That is untrue. Forget it.

It is forgotten.

Such an idea is foolishness.

It is stupid, said Alan, believing.

There are no aliens. There are neither supermen nor mutants. There is no thinking race on earth but the genus Homo. The accidents are unrelated; the welder a victim of shock, the pilot merely lucky.

I see.

The disks are under the supervision of the government, who wished to keep their purpose secret until now.

Security reasons, said Alan in blind agreement.

There is only you and there is only me, I who am you, you who are me. And this is our private knowledge and not to be spoken of.

I would die rather than tell of it.

Now you are mine again.

Never anything else, master.

Forget me.

Forgotten.

Go home.

Of course.

Alan rose and passed out of the range of the lights, and the tall man nodded with approval and began to switch off his terrible lamps.

ALAN woke in the grayness of dawn, cramped and half-chilled from sleeping in a chair. He stretched and groaned, and got up to brew some coffee. Brave woke at the clinking of china and came creeping out to the kitchen.

"Up so early, commodore? You look as if you hadn't slept."

"I slept, all right, but it didn't do much good. My head's splitting."

Brave took over the coffeepot.

"Any more ideas on the mutant theory?"

"Oh, hell. I guess I was wrong."

Brave turned and looked at him. "Why do you say that?"

"Well, look. The welder might have been suffering from shock. The pilot was—just lucky. And the business of the disks can be explained by obtuse government security regulations. And where does that leave our precious superman notion? Out in the cold and wet."

Brave shook his great head. "Huh-uh, son. More to it than that. Too many coincidences spoil the broth; too many queer things happening isn't right. I think you were on the trail of truth last night."

"I was talking through my ear," said Alan irritably.

Brave stared at him. A furrow appeared above the great hawk nose. He bent and pushed Alan's head back and looked into his friend's eyes. Alan tried to jerk his head away and Brave held it steady in the grip of one tough fist. He lifted Alan's lids one after the other and growled deep in his chest.

"What the devil, Brave!"

The Indian stood erect. "By the Great Spirit," he said. "Hypnotized!"

"What in hell's name are you talking about?"

"You've been hypnotized. Your pupils are swollen as big as grapes."

"You're crazy."

Brave regarded him equably. "Sure, tetrarch. Sure I'm crazy. Did you go out last night?"

"You were with me. What's wrong with you? We went to Win's."

"I mean later, when I was asleep."

"Certainly not. I did get up and go into the living room, though, and I fell asleep in a chair."

"Ah," said Brave. He considered a moment. "Watch the java, will you?"

Alan nodded. The Indian went out of the kitchen. Alan heard him moving things about in their little laboratory beside the plastiglassed lounging quarters. In five minutes he returned.

"Alan, you trust me, don't you?"

"My God, do you have to be reassured on that? Ever since we marched through Argentina together. Since Campana and Buenos Aires and that hell of Pergamino. I'd trust you if you told me to jump into Lower Bay."

"Okay. Now do me a favor." He gulped down a cup of scalding coffee. "Drink up and come with me."

ALAN drank obediently, and stood and followed Brave into the lab. In a cleared space stood a pair of machines, looking somewhat like giant cameras, the lens of one covered by a multicolored disk, that of the other unshaded; there were plastic charts bolted to the sides, and dials and several types of indicators, and among all these the distinctive green and gold seal of the Institute of Psychotherapeutic and Hypnotherapeutic Research.

Alan balked. "Hold on, Brave! You aren't going—"

"You said you trust me. Do it now if never again. Sit down."

"No!" he shouted. He was not quite sure of his reasons, but he knew he must not be hypnotized.

Brave moved to shut him off from the door. "You'll sit there if I have to knock you out, boss."

Alan saw he was not joking. He said, "Where did you get the machines, Brave?"

"Had them around for years. I've always been intrigued by hypnosis, you know that. In fact you knew I had the machines. Will you sit down?"

"What are you going to do?"

"Damn it, you're sparring for time. If you think—"

Alan swung on him without warning, a lashing buffet that could have broken a lesser man's neck; Brave took it square on the side of his jaw and staggered back, shaking his head. Then he caught Alan's coat as the smaller man leaped for the door. He swept him around by the coat like a yo-yo on a string, and judging his blow as carefully and dispassionately as an old champion measures an upstart contender, he rammed his big fist into Alan's belly just below the ribs. It jolted Alan back and doubled him over and made him blind with agony. He could not breathe. There was no air left in his lungs and he could not suck any into them. He was going to die. He wanted to die. He was dying.

Brave dropped him, unresisting, into the chair and tied him down with a few turns of a light rope. "Son," he said, "I know that wasn't you who socked me, it was whatever creeping louse got to you last night. I'll apologize later for smacking you...if you want me to." He went to his machines and began to turn dials and adjust gauges, and move pointers on the graduated scales. He tipped Alan's head up and clamped it firmly in the viselike apparatus that rose from the chair's back. Alan was groggy, his breath now hissing in and out between clenched teeth. Brave went on talking.

"I could have knocked you out, and it wouldn't have hurt nearly as much; but I wanted you awake. That pain may help, too. Rob Pope was saying something the other day about intense pain being an aid in nullifying the effects of hypnosis, when allied, that is, with counter-hypnosis. We'll see. Take it easy, pup."

Alan's technical training could be a deterrent factor, thought Brave. He may be able to oppose the mechanical-visual patterns successfully. Brave hoped not. It didn't seem to him that there was a lot of time left to them, and he wanted Alan back on his side.

HE focused the lens of one machine on Alan's half-open eyes and pressed a button. Light began to flicker across the agonized face, its color changing from second to second. Brave cut in the other beam and white light, which shifted its form even as the first shifted color, lanced through the blue and red and yellow. Alan shut his eyes, but immediately opened them again.

"You can't resist it," said Brave quietly. "You don't want to resist it. You like the pretty lights." The voice was an important stimulus too. "Your mind is conditioned to taking orders, isn't it, son? Somebody's been giving you evil commands. You don't like that. You'd rather listen to me." The weird patterns of the light beams held Alan's dull gaze. He was already adrift in a flashing vacuum, Brave's voice came to him slurred and without sense. Gradually he began to hear the words.

"Somebody hypnotized you last night, didn't they, son?"

"Yes. I think they did."

"Who did it?"

"I don't know. A tall man."

"Do you know his name?"

"I couldn't see his face very well."

"What did he tell you?"

There was a long silence. Then Alan, his face contorted, said, "He didn't tell me anything. He only put on the lights. They were vivid as sin. Then there was a voice."

"What did the voice say? You can tell Brave, son. Good

old Brave. You trust Brave."

He thought. "I can't tell you," he said. "Not even you. It was a voice. It was *the* voice. *My* voice. I love it."

"Isn't there anything you can repeat?"

"Yes. It said I had to forget the superman theory. It explained the accidents; and the disks. It's all natural. It isn't mutants."

Brave started to sweat. In spite of Alan's initial resistance, he pried his friend's mind, learning almost everything about the night before. But he did not find out that Alan had first heard the voice at the telecast, nor did he learn that the voice and Alan were one, master and slave, but one. The earlier hypnosis had been too clever. It had struck at the roots of Alan's soul, becoming religion and truth to him, and he would not deny it or betray it.

At last realizing that he had heard all he was going to hear, the Indian gave Alan certain counter-commands. He repeated them until Alan squirmed and whimpered under the repetition. Finally Brave was satisfied. By using the powerful mechanical-visual stimuli, it was usually easy enough to plant ideas in a subject, and only infinitely stronger agents could destroy such ideas. Brave hoped that the enemy did not have stronger agents; but he knew that in the last analysis it was a timid and unsure hope indeed.

"About all I can do now," he growled, "is stick with you as if I was a cocklebur in your hair—until they kill me, or we beat them."

HE turned off his machines and brought Alan to full consciousness. He untied him and led him into the lounging quarters, pushing him down onto a yielding sofa. "Take it easy for a while. That was quite an ordeal. I guess you have a bellyache." He poured two long Scotches. "Now tell me what you remember."

Alan thought. "Everything," he said with surprise. "At least I suppose it's everything." He repeated the substance of what they had both said in the lab. "Right?"

"That's it. I told you to remember it all. I wanted to level with you, chief. We've got a fight on our hands and I can't have you going around in a daze. You've got to realize what happened to you last night, so you can buck another attempt like it. By the way, you couldn't tell me why you went down to that building."

"I don't know. I haven't any memory of going, or of what happened there; I simply recall telling you about it. I have a memory of a memory, I suppose you could say."

"Strong medicine those dog soldiers are using," said Brave. "The more I learn about them, the surer I am that they're superior mutants."

"I think so too," said Alan.

Brave grinned. His therapy had overcome the former hypnotist's commands.

Alan went on. "The big question is, why have they suddenly appeared among us...why now? I think we have that answered. It isn't sudden; it may have been happening for generations. Slipups may have occurred as far back as history goes. One mistake might go unnoticed. Two might make a man wonder. Then he'd investigate and be either eliminated—they shot at me—or hypnotized and taken under their control."

"Bright lad! Your own experience bears that out."

"So the newest big question would be: how do we fight them? Perhaps we're the first to recognize them and retain our own wills. We can't let that circumstance go to waste, Brave. We've got to strike at them for our race's sake." He scowled. "But that leads to this: do we strike at them?"

"What do you mean, Alan?"

"I mean...well, Brave, would we be in the right to take law

into our own hands and start, let's say, a campaign of pinpointed murders against them? Suppose we were fighting good, instead of evil?"

Brave looked blank.

"How do we know they're wrong?"

Alan continued. "How do we know they're against us? Perhaps they are the true race of the future, and every man of intelligence should be on their side. No, this isn't an hypnotically planted theory: it's something I brooded on last night before I went to sleep. Where do our loyalties stand? If Homo superior is intelligent and self-centered, callous toward us, then obviously we fight him fang and claw. But if he is intelligent and benevolent, as you'd expect from a higher type of being, then we should ally ourselves with him."

"He shot at you. Is that benevolence?"

"I know. We might be wrong. It may have been a simple maniac who did it. Again, I think the coincidence would be too great. Well, perhaps Homo superior had a good reason for it. We can't judge too deeply on insufficient evidence."

BRAVE said, "I see what you mean, Alan, and in abstract theory I agree with it. If the mutants are a good breed, a real improvement on our own kind, then we owe them the allegiance of intelligent underlings. But concrete evidence says they're not good. They shoot at you; they employ the most malefic and vicious kind of hypnotism on you, where a simple conditioning to the fact of their goodness would have brought you around to their side just as easily—and with twice the value. They aren't good. They are villainous." He grimaced. "I can see you hate the idea. Why? What's on your mind that I don't know about?"

Alan turned a haunted face to him. "Brave," he said, "Brave, Win's one of them."

The Indian said, "No. You're wrong. Not Win."

"That's what I repeated a couple of hundred times last night. Not Win, not Win. But I mashed out a cigarette on her arm—accidentally, of course—and she didn't feel it. It left a hell of a burn. But she never felt it." She can't feel pain. She's mutant."

Brave laid his hands on his thighs and shook his head and could say nothing. Alan went on. "Has she been playing with me, then? Or can they get physical pleasure from us? Or was it her job to watch me for signs of awareness?"

"Not that. You've been engaged too long for that."

"Well, what is the reason? Is it possible that she could actually be in love with me? Me, a member of a lower species. I've asked myself could I fall in love with an orangutan? A fairly bright, good-looking orangutan? The answer always comes out no."

"Hardly a fair comparison." Alan glanced over at the mirror that formed the west wall of the otherwise plastiglassed-in room. He saw himself haggard, gray in the face, with bloodshot pouched eyes, and clad in tweeds that had obviously been slept in. "Hardly fair to the ape," he said, grinning a little.

"I can't believe Win is one of them," said Brave stubbornly.

"And I can't find any other explanation. If I make sure she is, and if we find they're evil, as we think, then I know what's the first thing I'll do." He looked his friend in the eyes. "I'll kill her, Brave. I'll cut her damned lying throat!"

THEN he stood up. "Enough of that. There are bigger things at stake than Win right now. I think we may take it as a truism that you and I can't hinder the superman's plans worth a whoop. Nor could we get to more than one or two people in authority before we were found out and stopped. Lord, the very ones we'd naturally go to are probably mutants themselves! So there's just one thing to be done. Enlist the fellows we know are all right. There's Don Mariner, for a start. He's plump and balding and looks ineffective but he's as smart a lad as we have on the Project. Then there's Rob Pope; he was in the hospital last month when he cut himself badly on a hot sheet of plasti-quartz. He's in the plastic chemistry section, but he knows a lot about hypnotism and such—like, so he'd be an asset."

"Can we trust him just because he cut himself? He might have faked the pain."

"Brave, we've got to trust somebody! All we can do is grasp at little indications of true humanity. Let's see. Who else is there?"

"Bill Thihling, the rocket jet man. He was at Oxford with me. Rhodes scholar, prince of a guy, and abnormally sensitive—I've seen him throw up when a dog was run over. He's no callous mutant."

"Good deal. That's five of us.

Any more?"

They thought hard. Mentioning names, discarding them as unsure risks, they ran through all their acquaintances. No more potential allies could they find till Alan said, "Jim McEldownie!"

"What do we know about Jim?"

"That he's uglier than the Duchess in *Alice*. Look at the mutants we've recognized: the welder, a well set-up Tarzan type; the pilot, a clean-cut handsome dog; and Win, a raving belle. Does Jim fit in with them? My sainted grandmother, no! And if we convince him of our belief, he might put us on TV to broadcast it to the country. *Worlds of Portent* has a huge following, and people believe what they see and hear on it. Then afterward, if *they* get us, we won't have wasted what may be the first and last opportunity men have had to publicize the presence of the enemy among us."

Brave went to the visiphone. There was an atmosphere of tense disquiet in the room now, as though things were about to burst out in violence and passion at any second. The Indian talked with Don Mariner and Pope and Thihling, who all agreed to come over within the hour. Then he called McEldownie. Shortly the lanky announcer was looking quizzically at him from the screen. "How, Lo." He shuddered. "How low can you reach for a gag? What's up?"

"Mac, can you get here right away?"

"Unholy cats—apologies to Unquote—why the rush?"

"Just say we need a good man in a hurry."

The other cocked an eyebrow. "I detect the aroma of butter, salve, and the old oil. Okay, I'll take an air taxi. Heat up any spare steak you have lying around. I haven't eaten breakfast."

"Naturally," said Brave, and turned off the visiphone. "There," he said to Alan, "now all we have to do is convince them."

IT took two hours to convert the four men to their views. Don Mariner, because of his own findings, was with them from the first exposition; Pope was intrigued but skeptical; Thihling was frankly incredulous, and McEldownie was scornful and astonished by turns. At last the fierce earnestness of Brave and Alan had its effect, and all of them were on their feet, pacing up and down, shouting at one another, smacking their fists into their palms and proposing unworkable plans at random.

Alan argued with Jim about the telecast. Finally the lean man said, "All right. I'm wacked. We're all wacked. They'll take away my job, my license, and my reputation. They'll toss us all in the booby hatch. Maybe we'll be lucky and get a room together. We can sit in a ring and make faces at each other for the next fifty years." He shrugged. "Nevertheless, we'll do it. We'll do it tonight. If things are coming to a head, we've got to step high and swift. I'd scheduled the Secretary of State tonight, but he'll have to wait. I'll go down and make arrangements. Won't say anything to the sponsors, naturally, or the staff. They trust me…they've done it for the last time, I imagine. Well, I've had five good years on TV. Let's finish it in a real crackerjack blaze of glory, gents. Here we go round the loony bin."

"You, boy," said Alan fervently, "are okay."

"I'm a living doll," said McEldownie moodily, and left.

Bill Thihling, the rocket jet man, a compact sturdy pocket-sized fellow about Brave's age—thirty-six or thirty-seven—said, "Now let's have some action. Let's *do* something."

"First thing we do is swallow some antigues," said Brave, going into the kitchen for the bottle. Antigues were anti-fatigue tablets, on which a man could keep fresh and intelligent for seventy-two hours without sleep. "I have an idea that sleep will be a myth and a vagrant memory for us before too long."

"And then," said Don Mariner, "we catch one of the supermen and beat some truth out of him."

Alan laughed hollowly, reminding himself of a character out of *MacBeth*. "Beat it out of him? Torture a being that doesn't feel pain?"

"Kill him, then," urged Rob Pope. "It's simple bloodthirst, but we've got to make a beginning. Perhaps it'll make his cousins fret a little. Bring 'em into the open."

"We don't even know they can be killed. A thousand-pound 'sword' couldn't faze the pilot of that disk. What could *we* do?"

"We can try! It's no good our arguing back and forth; we haven't any real data. The only thing to do is kidnap one of *them,* see what makes him tick, and then do our planning."

"I'm for that," said Don. "Which one shall we take?"

"The welder's vanished, and we can't very well torture, or try to torture, Win Gilmore. Too rough on Alan. Let's have in the pilot of the wrecked disk."

"He wouldn't come here if we called him—too suspicious a request," said Alan. "Kidnapping's the thing."

"Pope and I can handle that," said Thihling. "Anyone know his name?"

"Erin Grady," said Don Mariner. "Judas, isn't that a handle!"

Rob Pope, a big rangy man built in the style of a woodsrunner out of early America, said, "It's Erin Grady then. And if he tries any of his damn superman's hypnosis, I'll fling it in his own teeth. I know a trick or two in that line myself."

The two of them left the house. Brave began to mix three stiff high-balls and Don Mariner took out a harmonica and played Bach—with only a few sour notes per bar. Alan picked up the cat Unquote and fondled her, but his thoughts were grim. All he could see was a beautiful girl who he longed to hold in his arms. A beautiful girl with a cigarette burn on her arm. A girl who felt no pain. Win...

CHAPTER SIX

THEY brought in Erin Grady, dressed in brown civilian clothes and wearing an expression of curiosity on his lean well-proportioned face and in eyes that were accustomed to peering into measureless deeps of the sky. "How'd you get him?" asked Brave.

"Lied like a trooper," said Pope, and the pilot turned half-angry, half-amused blue eyes on him.

Brave gestured to a straight-backed chair. "Please sit

there, Mr. Grady." The pilot did so without question. "Forgive this wire," Brave went on, looping the heavy coils around the man's chest and arms, "but we don't think rope would hold you."

Then the pilot spoke. "Kept telling myself for years that scientists are all cracked," he said philosophically. "Guess this proves it."

"Bill," said the Indian to Thihling, "go out and patrol the house. Let us know if anybody approaches—anybody at all."

The rocket jet man left them. Brave put Grady's hands flat on the arms of the chair and lashed them down at wrist and knuckles. Then he stood back, Alan and Don and Rob a little behind him, and he said gravely, "Erin Grady, you smashed up a disk yesterday. But you weren't hurt."

"I was lucky."

"You sat in the regular pilot's chair as it hit?"

"Sure, I—" then his eyes narrowed and he shut his mouth.

"Too late," said Brave grimly. "You gave yourself away. You aren't so clever as you're supposed to be."

"Whaddaya mean?"

"For a superman, you're too slow on the trigger. We got into that disk before they clamped a security ring around it. We saw what happened to the chair. No human could have missed being sliced down the brisket by that juggernaut that came through the control board."

"You clever, clever little bastards," said Grady venomously. "You'll be dealt with." For the first time he seemed angered at the wire that held him. He threw his weight against it, but it held firm. He glared at each of them, and Rob Pope said, "He's trying hypnotism; watch yourselves."

Mariner chuckled. "He can't affect me, I'm too fat. The thought waves get lost."

Brave did not even feel the tentative vibrations of the

pilot's mind, but he glanced at Alan and saw that his friend was sweating. "You okay, guru?" he asked anxiously.

"He's talking to me." Alan's face cleared. "But I'm not going under. I believe your treatment did the trick, Brave."

THE pilot relaxed and deliberately spat on the rug. Brave reached out an arm like a tree trunk and slapped the tanned cheek, so the head rocked sideways. "We aren't going to be gentle with you, pal," said Don. "Face that. We aren't playing for marbles."

Grady did not speak. Brave took eight strips of light wood, narrow and about two inches long, from his pocket. Kneeling, he fitted them neatly under the pilot's well-mani-cured and rather long nails. The man flipped them out with a convulsive motion of the fingers; Brave impassively brought his enormous fist down like a hammer on the back of the fellow's right hand. Grady shrieked.

"Do that again and I'll break the other one," said Brave.

"You red-skinned bastard!" howled Grady, "you did bust it up."

"I meant to. I wanted to see if you'd be quick enough this time to simulate pain."

Had Alan not known better, he would have sworn the pilot was actually suffering. "What are you talking about? Why in blue hell shouldn't I feel pain?"

"Because you're a mutant, and we know you can't. Why can't you, I wonder," muttered Brave in a conversational tone, fitting the splinters under the nails again. "Pain is a necessity of life as we know it. It warns you of danger. A man could be sliced off up to the waist without noticing it, except for pain. Why would the next higher animal to man in the scale of evolution have lost the sensation of pain? It doesn't make sense."

"That's the first thing you've said that I agree with or

understand. It doesn't make sense. You're all nuts."

"Come off it," said Alan. "You have given yourself away too often. Don't go back to the old innocent routine."

Rob Pope said, "Suppose they can—regenerate lost appendages? It isn't as mad as it sounds. Suppose that welder slipped away and grew himself a new hand? In the case of such a beast, what good would pain be to him? It'd be no more than a nuisance. The lack of pain then becomes an intelligent development—but only then."

"What devils they must be," said Don, staring at Grady. "Right out of the swamps of Hell."

Brave said to the pilot, "Now I'm going to ask you a question. If you give me a fair answer I'll take out one of these sticks. If you don't, I'll drive it into you—under the nail it hurts about as bad as anything can—and light it. It's an old trick and it works wonders as a tongue-loosener. Here's the question: are you a mutant of our race, a superman?"

Grady looked at him for a moment and then he laughed. He was still laughing when Brave hit the stiff wood with a hammer and sank it beneath the nail. Then he screamed.

"You do that real well. It sounds as if that hurt you. Keep it up if you like; it won't bother me. I'm an Indian, Mr. Grady. I'm as sensitive and humane as the next guy until I'm up against somebody who fights unfairly, who is mean and cruel and treacherous; then I turn cold and I say to myself, how shall I fight this brute? And if torture is the best answer, I use it without any qualms. That's sense, it seems to me. Well, I hate your uncanny guts, Mr. Grady, and all your crew; and there isn't any way to fight you that I can see, so I'll torture you. And even if I'm nine-tenths certain that you aren't feeling it, still it eases me a little to hear you whoop and yell. And there's that tenth of my brain that says maybe you are feeling it. I hope you are. I really hope you are."

HE lit the wood—it was synthetic, a very light, hard compound of fibers that burned with a quick flame, as hot as the heart of a coal. It reached the nail and curled it back in two shavings of black char; and Grady almost shattered his throat with his roaring.

"Brave," said Alan, "stop it! He does feel it!"

"You raving maniacs, certainly I feel it!" Grady cried. "Where'd you get the idea I couldn't? You're all mad!"

Don Mariner said calmly, "I'll tell you why he doesn't feel it. Just look at his face." They all did so, uncomprehending. "He isn't sweating," said Don triumphantly, "and he hasn't even turned pale!"

Grady turned his head toward the engineer. "You fat little blob of stupidity," he said icily. "You stand there with your idiot companions and your bright little idea that's about as wrong as wrong can get. Of course I'm not sweating. *I haven't any sweat glands. I haven't any pores.* And naturally I can't turn pale. This is my natural color. I'm no damned human chameleon. But I can feel pain, in spite of your driveling theories. What do you want to know?" He spat again. "I won't sit here and take this agony for anyone. What the blazes can you do to us if you do know? You can't touch us. Go on, ask away."

"Are you mutants?" asked Brave.

"No."

"Are you human?"

"Not as you understand it."

"Where did you come from?"

The pilot sneered. "From the ninth planet of a sun unknown to you," he said.

Brave glanced back at Alan. "Think he's lying?"

"I swear I don't know."

"I'm not lying," said Grady. "Want to know how I got out of that disk alive? I heard the damn machinery shifting in front of me—oh yes, my ears are sharper and my sight's better, and I can move a lot faster than you can—so I spread myself out thin against the back of the seat. Lucky for me the monster stopped an inch short of my guts. Want to see how I did it? Will that convince you?"

Then he did an incredible, terrible thing to see. He seemed to turn almost fluid, and though none of his features changed, they withdrew to the sides; his whole body thinned out and flattened along the chair back, and he became a caricature of a man run over by a steam roller. Then he laughed at them.

Above Rob's gasp and Alan's cry came the shriek of Don Mariner. Then he had swept Brave aside and fired a grenade pistol almost in the face of the pilot; and Grady died without a sound.

"No recriminations," said Alan. "You can't see a thing like that and hold your hand. If I'd been armed I'd have done it myself."

Brave was running his hands over the exposed flesh of the dead pilot. "This is weird stuff," he said. "It isn't human— well, that's obvious. It feels vaguely like gutta-percha. It's swelling up slowly. No, by glory, it's going back into shape again. It's becoming humanoid again." He looked up. "Notice how that word springs to the mind? Humanoid. He wasn't human, he told the truth about that. He wasn't even superhuman. He was alien."

Don Mariner, still shaking, said, "I'm sorry I shot him. I just went out of my head at that stunt he pulled. Never been so scared in my life. I sure fouled up our chances of learning how and whom to fight."

" 'What can you do to us if you do know? You can't touch us.' " that was Rob Pope musing aloud. "What did he mean by that? That they're so powerful it doesn't matter now if we know about them?"

"You could put any interpretation on it," said Alan.

"Before we theorize any more," said Bill Thihling from the door, "you'd better know there's an air taxi headed this way. It's a Manhattan job and I thought it might be McEldownie again, but you never know. So what do we do with the corpse you birds so casually created?"

Brave said promptly, "The garbage disposal unit. It'll take care of him in thirty seconds—and very appropriate too." He hoisted the body of the pilot out of the chair, after cutting the wires. As he carried it off to the kitchen and the hidden well that was the disposal unit, Alan opened a camouflaged wall cupboard and took out the all-vac. Switching it on, he ran its round nozzle over the gouts and stains of blood on the rug, the walls, and the chair. It sucked them into itself like an anteater inhaling a hill of ants, leaving no trace of discoloration. Whipping it back into its nook, and tossing the long pieces of wire in after it, he slammed the door and turned round.

"That's that. We're clean. If it's Mac, we tell him the truth, otherwise Grady was never here. Right?"

Bill opened the door. McEldownie was just coming up the walk.

"Cheers, gang. The eminent statesman is put off. We're set for tonight. What crimes have you been committing?"

"Oh, kidnapping and murder," said Alan. The announcer dropped to the couch.

"You're jesting, I trust?"

"In a gnat's eye," said Mariner. "You're just thirty seconds too late to see the corpse." He told Jim briefly what they had done. The bony man did not say anything for a few moments, and then, "Jee-blinking-rusalem! You caught one and pumped him and slew him out of hand, all in the time it took me to fly to the studio and back. What a bunch of thugs. The Black Hand could take lessons from you." He leaned forward as Brave came in. "Well, you seem to have got precious little out of him before young Donald here got peeved, but let's coordinate it and see what we have."

"One, he could do miraculous things with his physical structure," said the Indian. "It's the first wholly sure thing we've learned since we saw the welder burn off his hand without flinching."

"Two," put in Alan, "he said his kind aren't mutants, but aliens from another system. It may be true. Lord knows. We have only his word."

"Three, he claimed to feel pain, and if he was faking, he was a class-A actor," said Rob Pope. "I'll tell you why: I was pretty sensitive to his brain waves, even when he wasn't broadcasting at us. Once I thought I caught a plea for help to someone unnamed. And every time Brave hurt him, I felt that he was actually suffering."

"I felt it too," agreed Alan.

BRAVE, getting out bottles of Scotch and rye, said, "In the minute I had to examine his skin and flesh, I found he wasn't lying about his being without pores. The skin was perfectly smooth. It felt rather like a kind of rubber, though not so much so as to seem inhuman to a casual touch. And his body assumed the human shape after death, so it would appear to be the natural form of the beasts." He passed one bottle to Rob and the other to Mac. The six allies drank deeply. Through two bottles they discussed the enemy; coming at last to a sort of half-conclusion, that there were extra-terrestrials who could change their shapes within limits, and there were others, either from the same strange world or existing as a mutation of Earthmen, who were impervious to pain. The aliens, Alan and his crew decided, were susceptible to it. The near-tangible thought waves from the tormented pilot had been too agonized to deny.

It was then a little past four in the afternoon.

"A bit more than three hours before we need to leave for the station," said Thihling, "if we take one of the colony's air taxis. What say we relax and forget for part of those three hours?"

Alan got up and went sprawling at full length on the deep-napped rug. "I'm for that. Let's loosen up. Loll around. I'm as strung up as Captain Kidd."

"I thought you fell down on purpose," said Rob. "But if you're capable of turning phrases like that, I guess you're just too drunk to stand."

Unquote found Alan and sat down with an air of modest ownership in the small of his back. Brave got out more bottles. "We ought to be drinking to things," he said. "There should be witty toasts and pledges to fair maidens. Bumpers should be drained to the memory of gay college days and friends long gone."

He passed the rye to McEldownie, who said, "We ought to be sucking this booze out of old ivy-covered pewter mugs, then, instead of giving each other our loathsome diseases. More collegiate, y'know."

The Indian took a healthy gulp of bourbon. He sighed appreciatively and flipped the bottle through the air and Bill caught it and had it uncorked and upended in the same motion, dexterous as a conjurer. "Ah," he said, choking and spluttering, "smooth!" He passed it to Alan, who nearly upset Unquote in reaching for it; the cat dug her claws into the rough fabric of his coat, glared at the back of his neck, and hissed sharply and at some length concerning the irreverence of certain men.

"Puss, simmer down," said Jim. "Your master drinketh."

"Now there's a bad word in its context," said Alan gravely. "You know nothing about cats, Mac. Nobody was ever a cat's master. If Napoleon kept a cat, it bullied him."

"Napoleon, my illiterate friend, had an intense fear of cats. So obviously he didn't own one."

"If Tamerlane had a cat, it bullied him. If Genghis Khan—"

"You've made your point. Send the alky on its way," said Don.

"Brave, pass around the old ivy-covered pewter mugs," Alan said grandly, rolling over and precipitating a furious Unquote to the rug. "While you're at it, get some old ivy-covered crackers and cheese."

"I could stomach an old ivy-covered potato chip," murmured Rob Pope.

"Let's have a little masculine nostalgia," said Bill. "Let's remember Oxford, Brave."

Four strictly American college men hooted him down.

BRAVE brought glasses and a tray of snacks, and, thoughtfully, a dish of milk for Unquote. "Here comes old ivy-covered Brave now," said Rob. The big Indian emptied a fifth of rye into the glasses. Jim picked up the empty bottle, regarded it like Hamlet with the skull of Yorick, and said, "Blessed blue ruin how I love thee. Omar had nothing on McEldownie."

"McEldownie the Tentmaker," said Alan. "It has a fine classic ring to it."

"I pawned my fine classic ring last week. I was hungry."

"Gad," said Bill. "Classic of '58, I presume?"

They finished the rye and after serious consultation opened a bottle of Scotch. McEldownie began to talk with a broad Highland accent and it seemed very funny to everyone. Unquote stalked away to her playbox in disgust. Brave sat bolt upright, looking like a statue of copper-colored granite. They all got drunk.

The announcer stood up and juggled three glasses, then

four, and the others applauded, for he was good at it. "For all your awkward look, Mac," said Alan, "you're a skilful old bird."

"When I juggled before the crowned heads of Europe, they went mad over me. I often wished I could juggle in front of whole people," he added wistfully. "Never did. Just heads."

"Oh brother," said a woman's voice. They all turned round and looked toward the door. Win Gilmore stood there, shaking her beautiful blued coiffure. "This place looks like a college kegger. And you're all fried to the eyeballs. Ought to be ashamed of yourselves." She dropped her lavender cloak. She was wearing an amethyst-colored halter and a pleated nylon skirt of syenite blue, which clung to her legs as she walked toward them. Alan could see the play of muscles in her thighs where the soft skirt touched them. Some of the liquor sank away from his brain and he remembered that this woman was not human. He gritted his teeth and turned his head away to look at Brave. The Indian was also sobered. He said, "Well, hello," uncertainly.

"It makes me mad," said Win, pouring herself a shot of rum. "All this attractive male virility going to waste. No women to appreciate it. There ought to be wenches flung picturesquely here and there."

"You paint a sordid picture, Madame," said Rob. "We've been chastely reliving old school days, knotting old school ties, and reciting the Boy Scout oath to each other. It's uplifting. It's—"

"Sophomoric?"

"Who is this dazzling fluff?" McEldownie asked.

"Win Gilmore."

The tall man opened his green eyes wide. "Oho? The super-jade!"

WIN regarded him without affection. "Who the hell are you, and what the hell do you mean by that crack?"

"Your secret is known, harridan," said Jim. He stared into her wide eyes. "Alan says you can't feel pain. That makes you one of the enemy in our book. If it weren't for your perfection of form, I myself would take pleasure in booting you in the left nostril." He let his gaze wander over her well-stocked amethyst halter. "Alan," he said critically, "far be it from ol' Mac to question your judgment, but I doubt this lassie's inhumanity. I really feel we've made another error. If she isn't human, then I'm a rhinoceros."

"You look more like a starving stork," Win cried furiously. "Alan, who is this wretch?"

"Peace, gal, I'm standing up for you, no matter what it sounds like. Doc, you can't convince me that a gal with a balcony that'd grace the Palace Theatre isn't human. I think you're wrong."

"Of course she's good looking. She's a step above us in the evolutionary scale, isn't she?" snarled Alan. "Or else she's from some damn planet out in the other galaxies." Win looked at him blankly.

"I think you've jumped to a conclusion when you should have crawled to it." McEldownie took a step forward and caught Win's eyes with his own. "I believe you can feel pain," he said.

"Good Lord, of course I can feel—ouch!" She gave a little scream. The announcer had pinched her sharply on the naked flesh just below her halter. Because she had been looking into his eyes, she could not have seen the casual motion of his hand.

"There!" said Jim, standing back and bowing with a juggler's flourish. "What about that, gentlemen?"

Brave spoke. "Win, he's drunk, so don't hold it against him. But he's done you—and us—a great service." Raising his voice above her passionate cursing, he went on. "You know our mutant theory. It's been changed today but the pain angle still holds good to a degree. Well, Alan burned you accidentally with his Rocketeer cigarette last night, and you didn't feel it; so we have been thinking that you must be one of them. Evidently you're not. You have our apologies all round."

She stood silent, taking it in; then she said, "Great heavens above!" and turned on Alan, who was looking sheepish and incredibly relieved. "You grunt-brain! Don't you, with all your knowledge, realize that there are times in a woman's life—yes, and in a man's—when she or he can be burned, whipped, and kicked in the funny bone, without realizing it?"

Alan made a gesture of incomprehension.

"You moron, what were we doing when you burned me?"

Brave reached into the encyclopedia of his mind and said, "She's right, governor. It was first explained way back in 1952. When one is sexually stimulated, the increase in blood pressure, the intensified heartbeats, and the rigidity of all the muscles sometimes combine to make one totally unaware of pain. The author of the theory was a Dr. Linsey, or Kinsey, or something like that." He pursed his lips. "I don't suggest that you were necking, chieftain, but if you were, that explains it, and we were damned unjust to Win."

"If you weren't necking, Doc," said Jim, "you're dead, or ought to be."

Win tossed down her rum. "I'll have more to say on the subject later," she declared to Alan. "For now, I'm too mad to risk staying here and breaking up the furniture. I found that burn on my arm after you left. By then it hurt like hell." She strode over and picked up her cloak. "Good night, or afternoon, or whatever the everlastingly blasted time it is," she said between her teeth, and closed the door gently behind her, which made a more effective exit than if she had slammed it and made the walls quiver.

"Bless my soul," said Jim mildly, reaching for his glass. "We have transformed a superwoman into a livid Fury. What a day!"

CHAPTER SEVEN

BRAVE passed around anticohol tablets, those excellent remedies for drunkenness developed in Japan in 1957; and they all ate them and drank water and looked at one another and grinned. "That was quite a bat while it lasted," said Don.

McEldownie rested his head on the couch and closed his eyes. Occasionally the tablets would put one to sleep for a short time. Rob Pope said, "We've had our reaction against all the shocks, and it was a luxury I think we deserved; but now we've got to plot and plan."

"The telecast is our first big hope. Let's put our heads together."

"And produce a sickening thud," said Jim, opening his eyes. "Okay we'll see what we can do. Or more likely," he said thoughtfully, "what we can't do."

The door opened and Win came in, a look of contrition on her face. They all gaped at her. "Well," she said to Alan, "it's like this. I'm sorry. I blew my cork. I was insulted. I'm not any more. I know the strain you've been under and I realize it was an awful coincidence to happen just when it did. I forgive you and your tame flamingo with the wandering hands. Can I help?"

"Take a pew," said Alan relieved beyond words. "We're talking out the telecast. You can help, sweetheart."

WHEN it was time to leave—they had decided to take

Rob Pope's station wagon rather than an air taxi—Brave locked up the house. Both he and Alan felt they might not be able to come back to it, at least not soon. Just before he shut the front door, a brown blur shot past him and landed on Alan's chest. Unquote clung there, claws entangled in his jacket, great blue eyes begging with false humility to be taken along. "I nearly forgot you, kitten," he said. He boosted her up to his shoulder and the eight of them got into the station wagon, which Brave then wheeled about and sent roaring toward Manhattan.

Just before eight they entered the studio. McEldownie said, "How about you lads waiting in the reception room? If anybody comes raging into the place for our hides, you can cause 'em a certain amount of trouble before they get to Doc and me."

Brave looked reluctant, then agreed. The others trooped out. Jim said, "You can watch it on the monitor," and locked the door behind them. "There's an extra precaution. Now for it, Doc. Cross your fingers."

The lights came on.

Alan talked well. Just at first, while McEldownie was giving him a purposely-vague introduction, he felt rather light-headed; this passed quickly. He had the feeling that something had tried to insert itself into his thoughts. Whatever it was, it failed, he thought thankfully. Mac finished his introduction. Alan began to speak.

He gave it to his audience straight and fast, without preamble, lest an engineer or official with access to the controls should be a mutant or alien.

"Listen to me. There are enemies among us, enemies from another world, or perhaps sports of our own species. We are all in deadly danger."

He spoke coolly and sanely. There could be no mistaking his competence to talk on the subject, he thought. He sounded like an old statesman.

After sketching in the incidents which had led to his suspicions, he told of the disks' unsuspected power, and of the pilot who could expand his body inhumanly in any direction. He did not mention Grady's death. He stressed the need for immediate action. "What that specific action must be, I don't presume to suggest. There are many men more qualified to tell you that than I am. But here are ideas…"

Seek them out, he said. Try to recall incidents or accidents that made no sense to you. Try to remember instances of lack of pain. I'm sorry I can't give you more identifying traits, but that's all we know so far. Except the lack of pores, the heightened senses.

There will be trouble. I feel sure there will be bloodshed. Don't quail, don't despair. We'll beat them. We're essentially a decent race and from all indications they are devious, malevolent, and evil.

And we outnumber them—that's pretty certain.

Don't flinch. Don't hesitate. Seek them out. Capture them, kill them, but *find them!*

He was really a little proud of himself as the telecast ended. He even felt light-headed again, and ascribed it to pride.

McEldownie clapped him on the shoulder. "Well, boy, if this mess pans out okay, you and I can take our pick of soft government posts, or retire on the bounty of a grateful world. Let's see what the gang thought of it."

He unlocked the door and opened it. Brave stood on the threshold, his dark face bewildered; the others crowded behind him, worried, tense. "Alan," said his friend, "what went wrong?"

Alan's belly shrank back and sweat broke out on his palms. "What do you mean, Brave? Didn't it go on the air?"

"It must have," Jim said. "I was watching a monitor."

"It went on, all right." Brave sighed. He looked as beaten as an Indian can ever look. "I should have guessed they wouldn't let you do it. They'd get to you some way, both of you."

"For the love of God, Brave, what are you talking about?" cried Alan. The other rested his hands on the scientist's shoulders.

"Son," he said quietly, "you talked about fuel. The two of you talked for fifteen minutes about the newest developments in rocket fuel. You never said a damned word about the enemy race!"

CHAPTER EIGHT

"So now we're all but helpless," said Bill Thihling, wiping his mouth. They had just finished three enormous platters of curried chicken at an exotic Bengali restaurant on 49th Street. "Where there's life, et cetera, but so long as the aliens control our very tongues, what can we do? Echo answers, Nothing."

"I blame myself for it," growled Brave. "I should have gone on the telecast; or Rob, maybe. We can withstand hypnotism, know how to fight it, while Alan had already had one bad dose of it. It must have been easy to recapture his mind."

"What about me?" objected Jim. "I've never been mesmerized before. I didn't feel a thing, either, or hear voices, nor nothin'."

"Are you sure you haven't been hypnotized? Alan didn't know it till I found out under mechanical-visual trance."

"Gad, maybe I have been, then," murmured Jim uncertainly.

"They got to Alan and Mac," said Rob. "Had you or I tried it, Brave, they'd have done something more violent; blasted the station off the air, killed us. They undoubtedly have their eyes on us, and we can't get in touch with humanity again. We're on an island surrounded by a sea of cynical, sneering demons; they won't let us do anything but make despairing futile signals to the mainland."

"Brother," said Win, "are we getting poetical in our sorrow! Listen, I have a feeling we shouldn't go back to Project Star. They must be grouping to wipe us out by now. They know us, they're not dumb; they'll be after us." She bent over the table and all the others did likewise. "Suppose we go up to Central Park? Sit out there all night and talk. We won't be hunted there. And perhaps by morning some solution will have occurred to us."

"That's the best thought any of us have had," said Rob Pope. "Fresh night air! I know this washed and filtered stuff is the best atmosphere for you, but I crave some real old-fashioned germ-polluted air."

So they took the station wagon up to the park, and walked onto the grass that was already spangled with moisture under the moon. On a knoll surrounded by trees they flung down blankets from the trunk of the car and stretched out and tasted the night that was brought to them on a softly brisk little breeze.

Alan said, "Mother Nature! You can't beat the old girl. She makes you see sparks of light where you know there's nothing but the dark."

They lay there and talked and napped and drank and relaxed through the night, till dawn rose gray and turned to blue and the sun came up. For no reason but their physical comfortableness, they all felt good. Even Unquote was gay and frisked like a kitten. Their fantastic trouble seemed smaller and further away than it had ever been...

WHEN the first great disk came down on the city, skimming the treetops of Central Park, heading straight for the Times Square district at that height and rising only when it seemed certain that it would smash itself against one or another of the buildings of Manhattan, none of them could speak for surprise. They stared up, amazed, as the whirling silver surface caught their eyes with its glancing beams of sun reflection; and it was incredible to them that the disk should be there in the bright morning sky.

It vanished over Brooklyn, tilting on edge and shooting straight up into emptiness.

"Well, if this isn't the feebleminded pinnacle of idiocy," exclaimed Don Mariner. "A test flight over the city itself! What drooling subhuman intellect ordered that one?"

In the distance a muted babbling arose, as the city caught its breath and began to talk excitedly about the flying saucer, the first (barring some fugitive glimpses starting back in the '40s that had never been properly verified) that New York had seen.

Then the disk came back. It led a wobbling formation, two sister ships just behind it and then a gap and three more, all going at a hawk-fast clip and slanting down out of the eastern sky to zoom over the park once more in an uncanny, wavering, noiseless line. Jim McEldownie leaped to his feet, his narrow face, with the green eyes staring out, a twisted mask of panic terror. Alan was shaken, as much by the lean man's fear as by the sight of the disks. "Mac, Mac," he shouted, "what is it?" For he could see nothing to dread that was worse than the thing they had been living with for the past hours.

Jim stared after the disappearing ships. "They aren't

ours," he said, his voice gurgling and choking with the fear. *"They aren't ours!"*

"Of course they are," snapped Brave. He too had risen, and stood like an age-old oak beside the quavering poplar that was McEldownie, "Whose would they be?" he reasoned. "Do you suppose any country could manufacture those things without our men on Albertus spying them out?"

"I tell you they aren't our ships!" cried Jim, taking the Indian by the lapels. "I know our designs up and down, and those aren't ours! Tell him, Mariner."

"He's right," said Don, white as paper. "The superstructure's all wrong. And they're bigger, I think, than ours."

"Don't forget that Homo superior, or his cousins from the space lanes, may have changed the plans without letting you in on it," said Bill Thihling bitterly. "By heavens! Nobody but a callous, egotistical mutant or alien, unacquainted with pain and insensitive to our safety, would fly a squadron of virtually untested disks over a crowded city. This is misanthropy with a vengeance!"

Mac groaned. "You bumbling dinkey engines," he said, "can't you get off that one track? I tell you these things don't come from Project Star—they don't even come from Earth!"

Win spoke for the first time. She was still seated, the cat cradled against her breast. "I think you're right," she said. "I feel it—you're right. Those aren't human beings in those ships. They're from black space somewhere. They know we are reaching out for the stars and they've come to stop us." Her tone was level and wholly undramatic. "We'd be a menace, rampaging through the systems. They won't let us begin. Their spies here, Grady and his ilk, have called them down to stop us."

Brave and Alan frowned at each other. Each asked the other wordlessly, Where are these two getting such wild conceptions? What do they see—what do they *know*, that we don't?

THE saucers returned, in a different formation this time, like a V of geese. Geese made of glittering blue-silver metal, round geese traveling at eight hundred miles an hour. They roared overhead: soundlessly, yes, but with so swift and terrible a movement that one could call it nothing but a silent roar. In that instant Alan, staring upward, felt his convictions dissolve. Mac was right. He did not know enough about the design of Project Star's disks to say that these were different; but he knew suddenly that there was an alien *feel* to these things, an aura of irrelation, a stupendous pulsation that pervaded the senses and forced the knowledge on him that here was nothing terrestrial, nothing human or even super-human.

Watching them shoot over, he tried weakly to find an analogy, to anchor his wits to some concrete remembrance and save them from scattering in panic. All he could think of was the night when he, aged six or seven, had wakened to know positively and without question that there was a ghost in the room with him. Even yet he was sure there had been a ghost. And this sense of alienness that came from the flying disks was the same as that he had felt in the night, when the invisible ghost crouched in a corner and moaned at him. An outsider, said his blood and viscera to him, a stranger from the cold hells of unknown space. An *alien,* said the wisdom drawn out of nowhere by primeval instincts lying in the murk at the bottom of his soul.

He moved to Brave and put a hand on one of the mighty arms and saw that Brave knew it now too. "Grady's kin," said the Indian. No one else spoke except Unquote, who gave a bizarre Siamese screech of rage.

Back they came, this time from the direction of

Richmond, in a strung out dipping line; and out of the crystal bubble in the belly of the leader there fell a shining golden egg, a tiny thing at this distance, seen only because the sun caught at it and played along its surface. It fell slowly, far too slowly for an Earth-hatched egg; Thihling and Mariner automatically judged its descent at six or eight feet per second. Either it was full of a light gas, or it had some form of antigravity mechanism attached to it. Leisurely it dropped toward Manhattan.

Then the people began to run.

All the millions who had been taught to act calmly and sanely in an emergency lost their heads; they were suddenly so many witless chickens who had caught sight of the axe. With the dropping of the golden egg, the terror of alien danger had clutched at them all. So they fled. There was no place to flee to, but they fled. Into subways and out again, insane with the horror of dying underground. Into buildings, to know the walls were collapsing on them, to run out once more. And the egg fell lazily toward them. Now it had passed the spire of the tallest skyscraper.

UP in the park, people were running too. Alan and his group stood together and watched them helplessly. "Like field mice from an owl," muttered Rob Pope. They saw a woman dash straight into a tree, carom off with a cry and go on. An elderly man came up to them, faltered, put a hand to his chest and pitched over at their feet. Bill turned him over. He was dead. "Heart attack. Poor devil."

Alan did not know why none of his friends ran. He repeated a random line that came into his head: "Stand and fight and see your slain, and take the bullet in your brain…"

Or the atomic blast, or the unimaginable projectile from the inconceivable weapon.

Then Jim McEldownie yelled, "On your faces, for God's

sake!" and Alan turned from the city and flung himself down and covered his head with his arms.

And the world opened up and a mushroom from Hell sprouted over Manhattan, and the buildings rocked and tottered and crashed to earth. The sky went black and the great white-yellow cloud, perimetered with blood-scarlet, arose against it; the universe shook and shattered and then came together and righted itself and sailed on. The Empire State was the last of the tall structures to hit ground. Clear at the northern tip of Central Park they felt that final smashing, a postscript to a letter from Lucifer.

From Fulton Street to 53rd, from the North River to Stuyvesant Town, nothing lived. In that terrible instant of fission, caught wherever they were, whatever they were doing, working at desks, peering from windows, running down deserted alleys or pushing madly against the press of maniac crowds on Broadway and Fifth and Madison, score upon score of thousands of men and women died; died screaming or weeping or fighting for breath, praying to their gods or cursing or dumb with dismay.

They died in subways, never having known that the silver ships of the enemy were sailing above their great town. They died asleep in their hotel rooms, lifting forkfuls of breakfast eggs to their mouths, typing words on paper, making love, staring at the sky.

Very few of them wanted to die. Some of them expected to live for many years. Some of them did not really expect to die at all. Many of them could accept the fact that death would come for every man in the world some day...except themselves; that was incredible and not to be thought of at all.

But they all died.

It came so quick, so quick; and even those who believed the golden egg to be a bomb never knew when it struck and smashed out at them and obliterated them, for the quickness was that of death, the swiftest thing that walks the universe.

Beyond the huge area of instant perfect destruction, many others died. Tall buildings collapsed on them, or they fell into the splits and great fissures that opened in the earth; they were hurled to the pavements and their brains spilled out, or the noise and the fearful rush of air got into their heads and tore their cerebra to tatters. Some of them could not bear the appalling horror of the bomb, and slit their own throats or put guns into their mouths and pulled the triggers. Some went so totally mad that their life forces disintegrated and they died where they stood, of madness and panic and the terrible knowledge of their impotence.

Men lived, too: lived blind and wounded and lamed and torn asunder, lived without minds and minds strangely contorted and warped. No one who had been in Manhattan that day survived without scars of body and brain left by the death of the city.

The golden egg had hatched its chick of death at eight-fifty-three of a Friday morning in June of 1970.

AFTER a while, when the hurricane had dropped away and the earth had stilled its shaking, Alan sat up and looked toward the heart of the city. The disks were gone—and so were the people and the buildings, the life and the fine aspiring skyline of Manhattan. Nothing was left but a leveled, broken, saw-toothed waste, over which hovered the direful mushroom cloud.

Grotesquely, irrelevantly, all his mind could focus on in that moment of near-insanity was his cat. "Where's Unquote?" he asked harshly. "Where's little Unquote?"

The cat spoke furiously above his head. She had flown into a tree at the blast. He coaxed her down as the others stood and brushed themselves off and stared at the atomic cloud. At last she bounced from a crotch of the tree into his arms. She was shivering with terror.

Bill said urgently, his voice no more than a croak, "Let's make tracks. Lord knows what scuds of radioactivity will be blowing our way soon, if that wind didn't bring them already."

"All those people," whispered Win. Now the screams and howls of survivors could be heard where they stood. "All those poor people."

"The wagon's liable to be stolen if we don't get to it," said Don. "Come on. Please."

There were still men and women running through the park, some shouting with fear, some white and sick and mute. A couple passed them, their eyes round and horrified, the man's coat torn and the girl's green dress ripped off one shoulder. They must have fallen, or been caught in a fight. There were two men brawling over by the reservoir.

There seemed to be no balance or reason left in mankind, save for the seven on the knoll, who clung to their sanity only by conscious physical effort.

Now they ran for the station wagon, to find its windows broken, the upholstery slashed by a knife, the windshield shattered. "Berserk," said Rob Pope. "They've all gone berserk."

"It does that to me, too" said Don. "I want to sink my teeth into something. I can't touch the enemy and so I want to take it out on something I can touch." He shrugged. "If you were lost in Hell, and found a car, and couldn't start it because you didn't have the key, wouldn't you get sore enough to wreck it? How are the tires?"

Brave said, "Okay. He was too mad to think of them." He knocked the remaining shards of windshield from the frame and got in behind the wheel. They all piled in. He started it and it rolled off northward.

McEldownie said, "No, Brave. Go down towards town. I want to get to a radio or TV station. We've got to try to establish contact with the rest of the world. This may have happened in other cities too." He leaned forward and put his hand on Brave's shoulder. "I don't think we need worry about radioactivity," he said. "These are beings from another planet, obviously much farther advanced than we are. Their weapons, though producing an apparently atomic cloud, would probably be without post-explosion danger. They'd have eliminated the radioactive dust because they'd want to land and take over at once, or at least quite soon. Let's take a chance. Let's go down toward Times Square."

BRAVE glanced back at him. The argument was specious, as a basis for action it wouldn't hold water. But Alan said, "I think so too, Brave. It sounds logical." Win and Don agreed. Brave looked at them. He was about to argue and then the fatalism of his ancient race seemed to grip him. They ought to get to a radio station, true; and if the city were radioactive, what did it matter in the long run? They were only seven people and a cat. Ranged against them on one hand stood the ranks of shadowy supermen and aliens, on the other the unknown disk-people. The world was in chaos. He could not dredge up enough ego to believe that he and Alan and the others would be very important in the ordering of that chaos. He shucked off his science and his civilized thought processes and he said, "All right. We'll go down." Stoically, the very incarnation of his thrice-great grandfather Pony Sees-the-Sky, he wheeled the car around and sent it hurtling toward Times Square.

Broadway was a shambles. As far up as Columbus Circle all the windows were gone, the light standards had been curved by the blast, autos were overturned and leaking gas and oil. There were cracks in the paving. Occasional men and women staggered along northward, and bodies lay in the gutters, across the thresholds. The wreckage of an air taxi half-blocked the way, corpses spilt halfway out of its doors.

"How many weapons have we?" asked Mac suddenly. "There's a sporting goods store. We ought to load up on guns. There's no telling what maniacs we'll be meeting, and if there's an occupation we might have to be guerrillas." He pulled back his coat. "I have a grenade pistol, for a start."

Brave had one, and an automatic for longer-range work. Don Mariner carried another grenade pistol. Win had her derringer-sized automatic in her purse. That was all they had. Brave pulled to the curb. He and Alan got out.

The store had lost its windows. Brave stepped through onto the display ledge and dropped inside. A voice in the gloom said, "Stand right there, mister." The proprietor, white and tense, leaned over his counter and held a .45 revolver steadily, its muzzle looking at the Indian's chest. "One more step and you join them." Brave saw there were bodies on the floor.

"I'm no looter, man," he said sharply. "I'll buy guns."

The fellow considered that. "By God, you sound sane. And you look like a good man. Everybody's crazy out there. You come back and pick yourself out something. We're going to need sane men with guns in this mess."

"Men are fighting each other," nodded Brave. "The blast drove them crazy."

"Can't tell me anything about that. One of those bodies was my brother. I couldn't let even my brother loose in this hell with a gun, not when he'd gone out of his head. Tried to kill me for a gun." The face was drawn and cold. "How about a .30-'06?" he asked. "Stop a grizzly if you're good enough. Heavy though."

"I wasn't looking for an air rifle," said Brave. Alan came in through the window. "He's with me. We have five others outside."

"You can have guns for 'em all. Sorry I don't have grenade pistols or flamers. This is a sporting goods store." He handed a .30-'06 across the counter. "Take this. I'll give you all the ammo I have for it. You put it to good use when the Russkis come."

"It wasn't Russians," said Alan, "It was flying saucers."

"Russkis in flying saucers. They'll be coming on the ground pretty soon. Didn't I see 'em come into Germany in the big war? Take these boxes. Enough ammo to stand a good siege here. Save all you can. We're going to be at war a long, long, time."

Shortly they came out into the morning air, carrying armloads of heavy rifles, four revolvers, and what seemed half a ton of ammunition.

The owner had at first refused payment, then taken only the wholesale cost. At the last minute he had given each of them a long hunting knife. "You were in Argentina, eh? You can use these. Give 'em what-for, boys." They had offered to take him with them. "I stick," he'd said. "This is my store."

THEY looked up and down the street. There were more people now, and the worst faction was evident—the looters, the sly lurkers who stole from the dead and exhausted and mad, the bestial men on the prowl for women, the ones who had gone lunatic and were bent on senseless destruction. A policeman, his uniform bloody, came toward them as they handed the guns into the station wagon; suddenly he whipped out his pistol and fired. A teen-aged boy came flopping and shrieking out of a store window, where he had been filling his pockets with candy and jackknifes and junk. The cop came abreast of them, his eyes lit with insane anger. Brave reached out and hit him on the jaw and he fell. "There was no call to shoot that kid," said Brave. He picked up the pistol and threw it into a drain. From up and down Broadway came scattered yells and sounds of gunfire.

They got into the wagon and Brave drove down to 57th Street. There was a mob of maddened men who fought each other and ran howling toward the car when they saw it. "Turn right," said Jim urgently. "There's a little independent radio station about two blocks away. With luck we can get in and out to the rest of the country. Unless that damned bomb smashed the place." They drew quickly away from the mob, which went back to fighting among themselves.

They found the station apparently safe; many of the smaller buildings here had been protected by the larger buildings from the force of the blast. With Don left to guard the wagon and guns, they ran into the place. The elevators had stopped. The men, with Win, trotted up four flights, to find a door marked with radio call letters. "This is it."

At the opening of the door three men turned swiftly from their work, grenade pistols and flamers—flame throwing handguns—in their fists. "Hold it," said the lanky Jim urgently.

"Bless us all," said one of the men, lowering his weapon, "it's McEldownie! What the hell are you doing in a *radio* station, Mac?"

"I'll eat crow for it, but right now I want to get out on the air," he said. "Can I?"

"God knows. We've sweat blood over the thing. Our own generators are okay, but the city's power is off, and the antennae got mashed up some. Couple of boys up on the roof now, worrying at it. Do you suppose we're loony for staying here?" he asked. Obviously he valued McEldownie's opinion. Alan realized for the first time what a reputation the scarecrow-like announcer had.

"No. There seems to be no danger of radioactivity; either

the bomb burst in air, or it's a new kind. We've got to get communication established as soon as possible. You're almost the only sane people we've seen."

"Most of our gang went out to try and get home. We're all bachelors and we figured it was up to us to stay." He ran a hand through his hair. "Who is it, Mac? Who hit us?"

"Martians," said Win.

"Venusians," said Rob Pope.

"Who are all these guys, Mac?"

"Scientists from Project Star." The three radiomen opened their eyes respectfully. "Pounce onto it, will you!" roared Mac. "We've got to get out. We've got to learn what's happened to the world!"

CHAPTER NINE

"Hi, Mac," said a weary voice. "This is Johnny Gibbons, in Frisco. No, they haven't been here, but they've hit half the big cities on the continent. Just heard that Mexico City's flat as a—my brother and his wife were in Mexico City. Vacation. To get away from it all."

"Cheers, Mac," said a deep sad voice. "Roscoe Toddy here. They bombed Chicago. Funny thing, some professors at Northwestern University here in Evanston turned their detectors on Chicago and couldn't get a whiff of radioactivity. Must be a new kind of A-bomb, or X-bomb, or GD-bomb or something."

"Mac," babbled a voice that verged on screaming lunacy, "Mac, you ought to see it. There's nothing left at all, not a thing, not a house or a tree, not a person in the whole place, nothing but waste, waste, death all over, I tell you the universe has gone mad!" They never learned where this voice came from, or what city was gone.

"Well, McEldownie," said a voice laced with intolerable sorrow and strain, "our station was partly wrecked but we finally got this thing in operating condition. Pittsburgh is gone, but we're out in East Liberty and didn't take too much of the blast. It was one bomb, Mac, one lousy big H-bomb or whichever letter they put on the biggest boom they can make. Mac, I'm beat to my socks." The voice coughed tightly. "I saw the Cathedral of Learning go. Good Lord, Mac, what a mighty toppling that was! It folded in and over and you thought it'd make a hole five miles deep, but it's lying there now, just a heap of busted stone, and I went to school there. Dear old Pittsburgh, Alma Mater."

A dark voice that spoke from far away said, "It was the maddest thing I ever saw. This golden oval thing fell about as fast as a feather, and everybody went out of their heads. We all started to run like mice. Cars were jamming Cahuenga and Sunset and Vine, and people were scuttling...I don't know why I wasn't killed. I just don't know."

"Yes," said a haunted and somber voice, "we ran. We all poured out into the streets and ran, and fell down and got stepped on and rose and ran and sweated and had heart attacks and died and lost our breath and panted and gulped and ran and ran and ran. Fort Worth is a shambles, a mucked-up mess."

"No," said a faintly insulted voice, "it wasn't a large bomb, not large at all. It didn't flatten more than four blocks. I was half a mile off when it hit but all I got was a skinned knee from falling. Hang it, why a large bomb on Los Angeles and only a little one on Toronto?"

"Seattle got it," said a smooth southern voice, "and your town, Mac, and L.A., and there isn't a peep out of Moscow but who can tell if they're playing possum? London is smashed; we're getting scraps from the hinterlands of England but London's had it. Paris is on the air. Johnny Jill, poor devil, is crying over there now, wanting to know if Hoboken is okay. We haven't seen the saucers yet in New Orleans. So ol' Manhattan got the guts torn out of her? Rough…darned rough. We're sorry."

"Austin's gone, gone, I tell you it's all all ALL GONE!" shrieked a slow-dying voice, and that was all it could say.

"Listen to this, Mac," urged a girl's voice, sounding strange and ethereal after the men had spoken so long. "We don't get how they did it, but those disks have thrown a force screen around every army encampment and station in the country, perhaps in the world. At Fort Bragg they mustered and marched out into an invisible wall. They can't penetrate it. It didn't hurt them, it just stopped them cold. Someplace in Pennsylvania the National Guard got into trucks and lit out for New York and ran into one of the walls that piled them up in heaps. It looks like we're all alone. Nobody's coming to help. We're all alone."

"This is London calling," said a cultured, horrified voice. "Hello, America. Can you hear me? We're not sure we're getting across the Atlantic. We haven't heard anything from you yet. Are you there? Can't you send us some word? This is the B.B.C. calling. London is gone. Bombed out completely. This is actually—actually Greenwich. Are you there? Is all America gone? Oh, this is ghastly, this is the end. Is it the end of the whole world? Are you there?"

CHAPTER TEN

DON Mariner, leaning out of the window of the station wagon as the band emerged, said urgently, "One of them landed. It landed just over there a way, I don't think more than half a mile. There aren't any others in sight. This one floated down not half a minute ago."

"What did I say?" exclaimed McEldownie. "They eliminated radioactive dust, so they could come right in after a bombing. It's logical."

"We'll go on foot," said Brave, "though I hate to abandon the car. But we'll have to go on foot over this rubble, and I take it we are going to the thing?"

"We sure are," said Rob Pope.

"Wait a minute. One of us ought to go with Win in the wagon and try to make it back to Project Star. She shouldn't be in this ruckus," protested Alan.

"You think she'd be better off out there with Lord knows how many mutants or supermen or aliens?" asked Bill Thihling. "You're not thinking straight, boy. We've got to stick together. Separate now and we may never see each other again."

"Besides, you can't get rid of me," said Win finally.

Don passed out the heavy sporting rifles, one to each of the men. They each had a sidearm (Brave two) and he and Alan had the wicked knives of the shopkeeper. Win had her little automatic for use in emergencies. Dividing the ammunition, and anchoring Unquote firmly to Alan's left shoulder with lengths of twine fashioned into harness and leash, they set off across the street; passed between buildings and across another street and yet another; and came to the area of near-total destruction. Here the going was precarious and tricky. Brave stared around them.

"Looks like Pergamino when we'd finished with it," he said to his friend.

A queer dead hush followed them about, muffling their footsteps and depressing them as though they crept through a graveyard. "That's what it is," said Alan half-aloud. "The biggest graveyard in the world." His hands ached to feel the throat of an enemy, to tear out the jugular, to slay and slay.

His world had been struck a fantastic, unaccountable blow, and it was dead around him and he and his friends seemed the only living humans from pole to pole.

They passed on, drifting quietly between broken crags that two hours before had been office buildings, hearing the echo of their light footfalls tossed back by windowless walls and heaps of brick and stone. One passage was clogged breast-high with corpses. They went around it, climbing over powdery granite piles that had been a theater's facade.

THEN there was the broad plain of ruin, a gargantuan bowl, smoothed down from its rim to the center, which was some twenty feet below the original level of the ground. Everything had been smashed here, buildings and trees and everything that stood upright; in the middle of the frightful desolated bowl rested one of the great silver disks, tilted like a gyroscope and balanced on its extreme edge, as though it leaned at its forty-five-degree angle against an invisible wall.

"That settles it," said Don. "Our ships can't do that stunt. Look, it balances like that and the bubble opened up makes an incline to the ground; fit steps inside the bubble and you have a perfect way of getting in and out. Our system is much clumsier. How the devil do they make it balance, though?"

"They've set up effective force screens around our armies," said Jim. "If they can do that, certainly they can utilize small editions of the screen mechanisms to hold up their saucers."

"Or maybe it's a principle of gyroscopics," added Bill.

"Well," said Brave, "we're going down there. At least I am. Anybody wants to stay here, Lord knows I won't blame him."

"We're all going."

"Okay. First Alan and Bill and I will walk out. If we aren't shot by the time we've gone twenty yards, you four come on. We can't plan anything till we get a look at the brutes in the disk; but as soon as we do, I'll shout out our next move. Is that all right with everyone? Or does one of you want to take charge ?"

"You're the chief, Brave," said Rob. "Maybe we outrank you on Project Star, but in action I'd back you against all of us. I've heard about you in Argentina."

"I didn't mean to assume command on the strength of my war record," said Brave seriously. "I simply figured I had the biggest voice and no matter what happens you'll probably be able to hear me. Okay, here we go. Guns at the ready."

They walked out onto the flattened waste that had been New York.

Nothing happened.

When they had been walking for eternity and six days longer, as Alan judged it, figures appeared below the huge disk, coming down the inclined steps or plane in the crystal bubble, grouping on the ground. The Earthmen were then just over an eighth of a mile from the ship.

The aliens looked human; it was difficult to see differences in their structure and that of a man; and they wore clothing that glistened as they moved in the sun. They were setting up three small pieces of machinery beneath the disk. Alan could not guess what they might be.

Then the men in the lead, Brave and Bill and Alan, ran into an unseen wall that knocked them staggering from the force of their own motion. The aliens had set up a screen around their ship.

"Here's where I yell out the plan, I guess," said Brave ruefully. "The plan is to make faces, men. That seems to be the only thing we can do of a warlike nature. A force wall! We might have known."

ALAN, who had sat down abruptly when he struck it,

jarring the tied-down cat on his shoulder and causing her to sink her claws through the coat into his skin with anger, stood up and felt the air before his face.

"Amazing. Touch this thing, you fellows. It feels like a sheet of hard rubber. It's perfectly tangible. I can almost feel a grain in the thing."

"What scientists they must be!" exclaimed Rob Pope. "This—hey!" he shouted, startled. "Here's an opening!"

Then he had walked on across the bowl. Bill Thihling, nearest him, tried to follow. He found there was no hole there. He skinned his nose on the force screen.

"Rob's crazy," he said. "He thinks there ain't no force wall there. So he walks through it. Only a loon could do it."

Pope came back. "I heard that. What the hell...? It was here a minute ago."

"Can't you get back?"

"No! The wall's solid again. By Jupiter, they let me come through; they wanted to see one of us at a time. All right, I'll play their game." He wheeled and marched straight toward the disk.

"Oh, Rob, come back!" screamed Win. "They'll do something awful to you!"

"Too late now," said Alan, taking her arm. "They've caught him in their cage like a rabbit."

"A fanged rabbit, anyway," said Don. "He's got his guns."

Rob walked under the silver ship, into its shadow. The aliens clustered about him. Beyond the wall of force, the men and the girl held their breath tensely.

After a minute or two, "Why," said Jim McEldownie, "they haven't even taken away his rifle!"

Shortly Rob turned his face toward them and waved. It was an encouraging motion. Whatever was happening did not seem hostile.

"And yet," said Alan to himself, "these are the devils who

smashed Manhattan. They *are* enemies." Even here, on the sloped plain that had been a roaring city, it was hard to realize it. He shook himself. Simply because they had not chopped Rob Pope down immediately, he had begun to slack off his hatred of them. He was growing tired and stupid. He reached into his pocket and took out an antique tablet and swallowed it.

Don Mariner, leaning heavily against the invisible wall, was abruptly shot forward to fall on his belly; the wall had vanished where he stood. Jim reached the spot an instant later, but the screen was whole. Don sat up, and his plump face was pale, but his grin was without panic.

"The Mariners have landed," he said, "and will shortly have the situation well in hand. Hold tight." He went down to the disk and the aliens.

THE waiting grew terrible in its intensity; Bill Thihling took his pulse and found it like a machine gun, even Brave sweated with anxiety, his dark fine face taut and frowning.

He was, as it happened the next to be admitted to the silver ship's area. Walking through the hole that opened to him, he thrust an arm back through it, trying to hold the force away till Alan had had time to follow him. Roughly, with a sensation of faint burning, the screen shut down and flung his arm to his side. It was like a sentient animal leaping from the sky to stand between him and his friend. After a moment's hesitation he went to the disk.

Mac came to Alan's side. "Listen, Doc," he said urgently. "Get your girl over here. The three of us are going through this thing together when our time comes."

"How?" And why, thought Alan. Is he scared to walk down over the plain alone? Why Win and me? How about Bill?

"I'll show you. Get up against the wall. I'll idle beside you and Win can stand on the other side. When it opens in front of one of us, the other two will jump like crickets and we'll go in, in lock step. Okay?"

"They may blast us if we disregard their obvious wishes." He gestured at the titanic bowl. "They can undoubtedly do it if we peeve them," he said lightly.

"We'll take that chance. I have an idea."

Alan shrugged. What they did seemed unimportant, the activities of a handful of fleas under a microscope.

The screen, as it happened, dissolved before Alan. More properly, he thought, it went up, like a sliding panel under his light-touching fingers. "Here it is," he said.

Instantly Mac had stepped behind him, one hand clutching out for Win's arm, the other around Alan's waist. Alan felt himself propelled through the doorway as if by a giant's shove; and the three of them stood inside, the girl looking rather bewildered.

"My Lord," she said to Mac, "you can move like an express train when you want to."

"Now listen," said the announcer. "When we get down there, be on your toes. Follow my lead. I know what I'm going to do. I'm—we're going to take over that ship."

"Jim, you're out of your head."

"No, I'm not. I know exactly what I'm going to do. We came here to smack these demons down, didn't we? Well, we will. Just be on your bloody toes, that's all."

Then they walked down the gentle slope until they had reached the shadow of the alien disk. They stopped a few feet from the watching outlanders. The captive Unquote writhed forward as far as she could on Alan's shoulder and spat at them.

They were a strange, a fantastic group, and yet they seemed to be human beings. Their bodies, much of which was unclothed, were built on the human scale; they averaged about six feet in height and their chest and limbs were developed to the same degree as a normally husky man's. Their foreheads were uniformly high. Their eyes varied in color, having irises of an unearthly hue, a kind of vivid violet. Only in the arrangement of their features did they differ perceptibly from the men of Terra: the cheeks were broader, the noses flatter, the eyes more widely spaced, and the bone structure much less apparent. Somewhere Alan had seen a man, lately, whose vague memory reminded him of these fellows. Where...?

Erin Grady!

WHEN the pilot, Grady, had spread himself out so to speak against the back of the chair, his face had widened, the features had drawn sideways and perceptibly flattened, so that he had resembled these saucermen. Was this what he had meant when he said, "You can't touch us. What could you do anyway?" This holocaust, this ghastly obliterating of New York and Los Angeles and fifty more great cities?

Grady had been a spy for them, a watcher, landed perhaps from one of the disks on a dark night...

He shook himself. That's romantic hogwash, he said to himself. Everyone on Project Star had a thorough checking-over, and his history from birth to the present was recorded in the files. That meant that Grady had been born here, in the United States.

Unless the keepers of the files were alien too, in which case a falsified record would be a simple matter to arrange.

But if he had been left here in comparatively recent times, say even four or five years ago, Alan went on, how did he learn our language, our backgrounds, our habits and customs and all the rest of it, so well? Are these creatures then so much farther advanced than we, that they can take on the perfect counterfeit of humanity in so short a time? He could not quite believe it. Grady had been too human.

Damn it all, *these* men looked too human!

He shrugged mentally, and began to examine their clothing. What there was of it was metallic, or of cloth that seemed metallic. Each one wore a wide belt of silver filigree, reaching up to the ribs and down just past the groin; beneath this a material that resembled cloth of gold, very soft and fine, was wound about the loins. They all wore sandals, of varying colors, the straps of which appeared to be made of tinted copper or a like metal. The rest of their outfits were evidently according to the individual's own taste; some wore arm bands of glittering orange or yellow gold, some had circlets of shining gray argent bound about their hair, which in all cases was blond and cut about shoulder length. The overall effect was splendidly barbaric, and about as far as Alan could imagine from the usual picture of visitors from space.

"They ought to have broadswords swinging at their thighs," he murmured to Win. "Or at least be toting horn cups full of mead."

"Aren't they something!" she said, and then, "are these the devils who bombed all our world a few hours back? These big good-looking boys? I can't believe it."

One of them bent over a square steel-like box and turned a dial; they heard Bill Thihling shout in the distance, "Hey, the wall's gone!" and saw him come running toward them.

"They're the ones," said Alan, and his mind, occupied till now with the romantic appearance of the invaders, became filled with hate.

INSTANTLY he felt something probing into his thoughts. It was, although he did not remember it, very like his first experience of hypnosis during the telecast. All he knew now, however, was that someone was leafing through his emotions and ideas as if they had been a large plainly printed book. It made him furious. He might have done anything, shouted angrily or struck out at the nearest alien in an access of physical passion; but it was then that Jim McEldownie made his move.

"Okay," the lanky man roared, "strike now! Blast 'em! Get into the ship!" He lifted his rifle and fired it from the hip, and one of the outlanders spun round and fell, a great bloody cavern torn in his chest.

Alan did not question Jim's methods, though two minutes before he would have; he blew the head off the nearest blond saucerman and shot over the falling body at another. Brave fired too, and Don Mariner; the others were caught by surprise and only stared wide-eyed.

An alien drew a silver tube from the back of his filigreed silver girdle and from its tiny muzzle a gout of scarlet flame flew at Alan. He felt nothing, thanked his luck that it had missed, and shot the man through the head. Then he was racing after McEldownie toward the crystal bubble's inclined plane.

Up they went into the disk, he and Mac in the lead, Unquote hissing murder on his shoulder. Behind them he could hear the others pounding along, crying out questions or vague threats or battle cries.

The ship was much larger than those of Project Star, and more complex within, the ramp reached to a corridor with three doors. Mac was dashing for the farthest one; Alan threw his weight against the middle door. As it burst open his first glimpse was of four outlanders rising, open-mouthed, from chairs set before a bank of control panels.

Afterwards he could recall only the thing that flashed through his mind in that first instant of viewing them: that in the old West it had been proved time and again that one good man with a repeating rifle was better than four good men with revolvers. Alan proved it now, not against guns, but against the small silver tubes that spat flame balls. The room was a shambles in eight seconds, and Alan turned for more conquest, to stumble over the body of a man in the corridor.

IT was Don Mariner, and he had no face. There was a raw, bloody burn from ear to ear, from brow to throat. He had probably died very quickly. Alan straightened and gripped his gun's stock till the fingertips splayed out white and flat against it. Old Don, he said, old plump Don. Not so old, he said, probably no more than forty-two or forty-three, but you always thought of him affectionately as Old Don. Now who will there be to exclaim "By Judas!" when things get tough?

"Brave!" he bawled out. "Brave, are you safe?" He was hideously afraid for his great friend. When the copper face peered out of the third door, he was ill with relief.

"Had a little dust-up in here," said the Indian. "These boys wanted to brawl, by gosh," he said, coming out, "Don's had it."

"Yes, he's had it."

"He was a good man. Did we lose anyone else? I think the saucermen are all through."

Jim McEldownie joined them. "The big control room's up front there. We killed seven of 'em there. Rob took a leg burn and he'll walk with a limp for a while. No more casualties."

"Those tubes of theirs are frightful. If we hadn't taken them so by surprise—"

"They were too careless," said Brave. "Doesn't make sense."

Rob Pope hobbled out, one arm over Bill's' shoulders. "I think I know why," he said. "When they got me down here, they searched through my mind. I could feel it plain as a physical touch. They found hate there, I'll be bound, but it was for the bombing of the city, not a congenital hatred of outsiders. They found the same in Bill's mind. It relaxed them and put them off guard."

"How do you figure that?" asked Win.

"They were looking for an ingrained enmity toward themselves. It astonished them when they didn't find it. They're tremendously telepathic, and I'll wager hypnotic too. I think they do much of their own communicating by thought waves; at least I didn't hear them speak once.

"When they discovered why I was angry, they were stunned. I mean they were shocked. You see, they made a mistake. They realized that as soon as they'd pried into my mind. They thought we were down here just waiting to kill them as soon as they landed, and naturally they had to cripple us before they dared do it. Then they found out their mistake. They had to kill someone, I'm not sure who, but the bombing of our cities could have been avoided had they known what we were like."

"Wait a minute," objected Brave. "Rob, how do you know all this?"

Pope looked surprised. "Why, they told me. They had just begun to explain it, hardly got more than a few ideas across, when you and Mac and Alan busted loose. If I'd known what you were planning I'd have stopped you. But now we have made a mistake as bad in its way as theirs."

"They told you all this?" asked Win blankly.

"Yes. They talked in my mind. Not in English, but it came out that way. It was—pictures, I suppose is the nearest thing to it. Emotions and both abstract and concrete ideas can be transmitted by a good telepathist; and these boys were the best." He shook his head. "It's too bad. God knows where it will all end now."

CHAPTER ELEVEN

THEY carried the body of Don Mariner down the ramp and laid it on the rock-hard earth of the desolate bowl.

Mac, standing next to Alan, said in his ear, "Come aboard again. I want to show you something."

Alan turned obediently, although why he should follow Mac's commands—for it had been a command—he wasn't sure; and Win screamed, a high hysterical keening that set Unquote to ululating too. The men all cried out. "What's wrong? What is it?"

"Look at your head!" she said to Alan, pointing. Even in that somber moment he could not help laughing.

"How?" he said. "I'm not built that way."

"Good Lord," said Bill Thihling. "Alan, you took an awful blast in the ear. Why didn't you say something about it?"

"What are you talking about?" he said irritably. "I wasn't hit." He put a hand up to his right ear. Brave said, "Look out, boss, you'll hurt it. It's a bad one."

He fingered the ear. The tip and lobe, and part of the convolutions of the outer ear, felt like bits of steak which had been burnt in a searing flame; he looked at his fingers, amazed, and saw black flakes of skin and powdery, charcoal-like stuff. That must be the flesh, cooked and carbonized, almost incinerated in the astounding heat of the little fireball. "They did hit me," he said stupidly, staring at his fingers. "I never felt it."

Brave, examining the ear without touching it, said, "You'll lose most of that ear, son. It's—*you never felt it?*"

"I can't feel it now. I mean, I have sensation in it, I can feel my fingers when they touch it, but it doesn't hurt."

Then, just as comprehension of what he was saying began to dawn on him, he heard Mac say again, very urgently, "Get aboard the ship. Jump!" And he jumped.

He hurried up the ramp, Unquote writhing on his shoulder, and leaped in through the first door he came to; Mac yelled, "No, this one!" It was the front control room, the largest of the three; he was out and into it in a flash, to find Mac already sitting in a chair before the central panels. "Sit down there," snapped the lanky man, indicating the next seat. Alan did, half-wondering why, half-knowing that he must. The great view-plates above the controls, on which were mirrored the earth and sky on every side of the disk, blinked on; Mac cursed angrily.

"Why couldn't you have followed me at once? Now the fools have got in." He was out of the chair and bolting the door of the room before Alan could open his mouth. Then he was back, touching levers and buttons, adjusting dials. One of the view-plates showed the crystal bubble closing; then another came on and they could see the center room. Brave and Win and the others were there, talking earnestly, although their voices could not be heard. Suddenly the door to that room swung shut. Brave hurled his tremendous bulk at it, but it was shut fast. Mac chuckled.

"Okay, you damned impetuous idiots. Sit down if you don't want to be smeared all over the floor." Evidently they could hear him. After a moment's argument they took seats. Mac pushed over a long lever, like the joystick of a monoplane, and with a very slight rocking motion the saucer rose into the air.

MAC glanced at Alan. "Buckle that strap around your chest, pal. You'll need it for the turns."

"How in the name of everything sane did you learn to operate a disk, Jim?" he asked. Just then he was less surprised at the man's cavalier treatment of his friends than at the enormity of this, that McEldownie could fly an alien disk.

"Nothing to it," said the other. "I was a pilot originally." He looked over again. *"That was five hundred years ago,"* he said, almost casually. "Buckle the strap, hang it."

Alan did so in a daze. He knew that he was not in complete control of himself, and yet he did not know why. There were a hundred questions rocketing in his mind and they confused him so that obedience to McEldownie's commands came automatically. He wondered if he was under hypnotic influence again; but he did not feel that he was.

"Oh, you are, chum," said Mac without looking at him. "Not altogether, you understand; Brave's counter-hypnosis played hell with my plans for you. Cuss the big so-and-so. I should have killed him when he moved out of the lamps and out of any possible control. But I wanted him too. I liked him."

"Who are you?" breathed Alan.

The cold voice spoke in his mind, shattering his questions before they were asked, shaking what was left of his confidence, forcing him to quail mentally and physically.

Oh, stubborn slave, didn't you know? Didn't you know?

God, God, perhaps I did.

I am you and you are me…

McEldownie laughed. It was not a cold laugh, not sinister or dramatic. It was a perfectly healthy expression of mirth. "Alan, I'm sorry. I'm really sorry, and you won't ever believe that, but it's true. It surprises me. Living among you for all these years has mellowed ol' Mac, I guess. I find myself thinking of you as friends, when I used to regard you as dogs: faithful without knowing it, helpful, indispensable in many cases, but hardly more than good dogs." He paused a moment, then went on. "I'm your voice, of course. There's no trick to it when you know how. A matter of hypnosis plus the lights plus psychology, plus whatever the power in us is that makes our minds different from yours. I'm the voice. I wasn't going to admit it, but my plans have changed for you."

HE banked the disk around over desolate Manhattan and said, "Takes a while to get the reflexes working again. I haven't sat behind the controls since we left home. Your five-times-great grandfather wasn't a twinkle in his old man's eye when we left home."

Alan could not speak. He was remembering things he had not been able to remember, the voice and what it had told him, the night that it called him from bed to come to the terrible lamps, and—

"Yes, it was me, it was all me, Alan. I was the voice in your head at the telecast, I called you in the night; I worked the lights in the shed on Project Star. There are plenty of us out there, but I wanted you for my own personal sidekick. You're smart and a good scientist, and you'll make a good lieutenant when we go home." The words made no sense and yet Alan seemed to catch a glimmering of the understanding that was to come.

Alan said, "I guess I ought to exclaim, 'You're mad!' but I know you're not. You can pilot this thing and you can move faster than a cheetah, and everything's gone mad this past week and I want to know why. Don't lie to me, Mac. For the love of God, don't lie to me. One more wrong theory implanted in my skull and I'll blow my stack for good."

"I won't lie. I'm all through lying—to you at any rate. The others can't hear me at the moment, but I suppose I may as well tune them in too." His homely face, with its great prow of a nose and the half-shut green eyes, looked a little sad. "I'm afraid they're all going to die, Alan. Except Win, that is. You see, the speeds at which I'm going to fly this disk will kill a human being. On the turns, if I get into dogfights, the 'G' forces will be terrific. You and Win can stand 'em, because you've been conditioned. Brave and Rob and Bill will be smashed to jelly under the 'G' impact. I'm sorry. I like Brave and I admire Rob's intelligence. I'd like to save them. But they got aboard because you were slow, and now they're done for. I can't land and put them out. Time is precious. I have to maneuver this ship until I know I can do stunts with her like the ones I did at home. A long time ago, Alan." He grinned ruefully. "A long time even to me."

"What do you mean, I was slow getting aboard?" Alan fastened on this small facet of the affair, frightened of finding out too much of the truth at once.

"Man, you can move as fast as I can if you try. You've had three long treatments under the lamps. Your energies are stepped up, if you learn to use them correctly, your reflexes are as fast as those of the cat on your shoulder, and you're almost deathless compared to your friends. Might as well start there," he mused. "They can hear us in the other room." On the view-plate, Win and Brave nodded. Jim clicked shut a switch. "Now they can see us. Okay, you four, I'm going to do some explaining. I can hear you now, but if you start to interrupt I'll switch you off."

Brave said, "Alan, are you all right?"

"He's ginger-peachy," said Mac. "In fact he'll be all right two hundred years from now.

"There's no use in explaining the rays to you; it would take hours and you would scarcely grasp the principle even then. I'll tell you what they do. They lengthen your life span—my own is about a thousand years, but Alan's will be nearer four hundred, for I caught him late. Generations of my ancestors were exposed to them, too; it affects the genes eventually and we're born long-lived. They quicken your reflexes through a process of strengthening the nerves and certain cells of the brain. They also affect the portions of the brain that send and receive telepathic stimuli. After one treatment it's easy to control a man over a long distance.

"The effect of the rays on the muscles is unique. They become almost rubbery, not loose, you understand, but capable of stretching and flexing in directions that look uncanny to a non-initiate. That's how poor Grady escaped being sliced down the middle when he rammed up his ship. He drew all his muscles to the sides and flattened out like a plaster on the chair. You couldn't do that. Your skeletons are thicker and more immovable than ours. I'd show you how I can ooze out sideways and make my ribs about as level as a picket fence—but I'm afraid you wouldn't like the sight. It must be pretty gruesome to an Earthman."

"Were the rays in the TV lights?" asked Bill Thihling.

"That's right. I've caught plenty of fish that way, including United States President Blose and nine-tenths of his cabinet. A lot of your scientists have become unwitting puppets through being seen on *Worlds of Portent*. Alan got two treatments there and one on Project Star. Win got her first in the gym of the colony and two more in that shed." He smiled guilelessly. "You were right about her, of course, in a way I mean; for she can't feel pain. I caught her mind just before I pinched her—and very pleasant it was, too, my dear, even if I meant it impersonally—and told her to simulate pain. She was under my control every second of that time. When she left, I pretended to go to sleep, and called her back. I had a feeling I'd need her around. Glad I did. She and Alan are all the fighting forces I have at the moment."

ALAN brushed over much of what he wanted to know, to ask, "Can you feel pain, Mac?"

"Yes, I can. A man can't give up pain. It's too valuable. We put an added ingredient in to the rays we used on you people of Terra, to eliminate pain."

"Why?"

"I'll get to that. The welder, of course, was a man who had been treated. One of our boys got rid of him in a vat of molten metal. Couldn't have an unfinished experiment walking around loose. He slipped up when he failed to simulate pain. Sometimes we get 'em like that, too dumb to do the right things even under complete hypnosis. Win was a different case. She didn't know she'd been burned by that cigarette. If she'd seen it, she'd have yipped. She was conditioned to do it, even to think she felt pain. If you'd known you'd been grazed by that fireball, Alan, you'd not only have roared, you'd have *thought* you felt it."

"Why don't I think so now?"

"It's too late for verisimilitude. Your subconscious knows that. It shrugs its teensy-weensy shoulders and forgets it."

"Who shot at Alan after the welder incident?" asked Brave. His face was cold and malignant.

"One of Getty's men."

"Doc Pomposity?"

"That's right. Getty's not fully under control. His unconscious and natural wish not to kill Alan made him send a man out with an automatic, rather than a grenade pistol. But he was conditioned enough to feel that Alan was dangerous to us and he at least made a stab at assassination. Then before he could do it again, we got to him and told him we were going to 'convert' you."

All this while Mac was twisting and turning the disk, making practice runs and dives. The control rooms, floated within the hull and leveling off no matter what direction the great saucer took, vibrated slightly and continuously. It was almost like being in the hold of a sailing ship.

Rob said, "I suppose the curious construction of your skeletons and muscular development helps you stand the motion and the acceleration of the disks?"

"That's right. Alan and Win can stand it too, especially since they feel no pain of any sort. But we haven't started going fast yet—I haven't put it above five hundred. When we hit four thousand—that's M.P.H.—I'm afraid the three of you will die." Mac scowled unhappily. "I hope you realize I don't want to kill you? In the first place, I'd like to have you on my side, because we both have a score to settle with the hounds who bombed your cities. I would have slain Mariner out of hand, slain him as he slew poor Grady when he had him helpless in that chair, but luckily he got his in the fight. I haven't any wish to kill off my potential army, but the speed of an air battle will do it. And I'm going to be in some fights before long."

Alan, strapped to his chair, was leaning over toward Mac as far as he could. Now he said, "By heaven, you haven't any pores in your skin!"

"I was afraid you'd notice that before. I had a fantastic yarn cooked up to explain it. That's right, pal. Grady and me, and all the rest of us, haven't any sweat glands or pores or tear ducts. There are other little differences too, but they don't cut any ice. The differences notwithstanding, we are human. Not strictly Earth-type human, I suppose, but human nonetheless." He brooded over his controls, as the disk roared silently through the sky. "I like you all, too, dammit. I don't want to kill you. I think I'll chance another ten minutes and set you down.

"I must be getting soft in my middle age," he added with a wry smile. "Chancing the loss of a world for three idiot kids. Oh, well. What the hell. A gallant gesture will maybe pay off in the long run."

THERE were several minor points that nagged at Alan; he wanted them out of the way before someone asked the one big question of McEldownie. "Why didn't Grady control my mind when we tied him up? Why couldn't he save himself?"

"Erin Grady was a weak link. We have them in our chain, you know. We're not supermen. He was weak at hypnosis and he couldn't bear pain. I think he was a throwback to the days when we were altogether Earth-style humanity. He called to me, though, and I shot back; but I came just too late. That fool Mariner!" With a savage twist he angled the disk toward earth. Then he laughed. "I've wanted to compliment you on your mutant theory, Alan. It was ingenious as the devil and it accounted for everything you'd seen up to that time. If we could regenerate parts, the loss of pain wouldn't matter, and we could take the treatment we're giving you and lose pain and be thankful. But 'tain't so. We're not supermen. It's only our robots—pardon me, our earthly henchmen—who are immune to pain. Coming in contact with both kinds of 'aliens' must have confused the very living dickens out of you."

"Hold on," said Alan. "I just thought of something. If I'm immune to pain, why did I feel it so excruciatingly when Brave hit me, when he wanted to put me under hypnosis? Tell me that was all in my mind...!"

"It wasn't. You didn't get the pain-destroying rays till your third treatment, on last night's telecast."

"So that's it." He patted Unquote on the head; she was getting restless. Then it became obvious why. "Damn," said Alan, "now I'll have to have this suit cleaned. Puss, couldn't you have waited a little longer?"

Bill asked, "What about the saucers? I mean, they suddenly turned out to be better than anyone suspected. Why?"

McEldownie looked grim. "Some saucers had been sighted that we knew weren't ours. We had a few left from the days when we first came to Earth, in the late 1700s; we used to fly 'em occasionally to keep our hands in. But these weren't ours. So we knew we had to speed things up. Until then we'd been content to go along, giving your scientists an unobtrusive push now and then, so they'd believe they had done it all; our time schedule called for intergalactic space disks about 1984. Well, we knew when the others were seen that we didn't have all the time in the world, as we'd thought. So we had to jump in feet first, take a lot of men under our controlling wing, start making robots—there I go again, that's a bad word for them—making unkillable soldiers of others, and substitute our own advanced designs for those in use at that time. We were too late; the damned enemy came down too fast. But now that I've got one of theirs—and a beauty it is, too—thanks to your help, I have a fighting chance."

"Who are the enemy?" It was Win, breathless, leaning forward, her breast rising and falling rapidly with the emotion and wonder of this thing. "Who are you going to fight?"

Mac looked at her in the view-plate. "The men from my planet," he said quietly. "The men who cast us out, as if we'd been the fallen angels of Lucifer in your myth, chucked us out of our own world and sent us to wander in the void."

HE made the ship do a quick turn, and Alan saw Brave and Rob and Bill suck in their bellies and grimace. Mac said, "They half-crippled me then, damn them, and this is the first time I've flown since I left home. Some of the others have managed to stay a little more in practice. But by God, I'm still the best hotshot pilot my people ever produced, and I'm going to prove it today." He glanced up at the view-plate. "I'm going to let you out, you three. I want Alan and Win. They're my people now, and in a fight they can be a terrific help, for they're almost impossible to kill. I'll land now, and you can go. I oughtn't to do it. But curse you, my Indian friend, I like you." He shot the disk toward the earth from a height of seven miles.

Brave said, "We won't get out."

"Don't be silly. You'll die under the 'G' load when I really get going."

"Then we'll die. I won't leave Alan with you, nor Win either. You will let us all out, or kill us."

"You bloody village idiot. What good will it do you to die?"

"I can't leave Alan. I saw him through Argentina and I'll see him through this hell you've put him into. Besides, someone's got to clean and bandage that ear, or he'll lose the whole thing. It's a bad wound."

"Not to him it's not. He doesn't feel it. The rays eliminate all danger of infection, disease—he can't even catch a common cold. His ear will be okay."

"Ear, schmear," said Rob Pope. "I stick by my friends too. Maybe, all I can do is die like a squashed mouse, but I *can* do that. We don't scuttle for cover, alien."

"Likewise," said Bill Thihling laconically.

"Beastly blasted blue-bottomed baboons of knot-headed numbskulls!" roared McEldownie. "Do you want me to kill you, then?"

"I want you to let us all go; but if you won't, then Alan's better dead than living under your influence, like a marionette."

"He won't die. I tell you! No matter what happens to you, he'll go on living. He'll be my man."

"I don't think so," said Brave calmly. "I don't care what sort of all-powerful rays you put him under, or how you've caught the reins of his mind. If you kill me, Alan is sooner or later going to kill you. Live with that, McEldownie, or whatever your right name is. I don't for a minute believe that you can take as good a man as Alan and murder his best friend before his eyes and have him lick your boots. Kill me and you're done, Mac."

"Damn you, Lo! You're wrong, and you know it." He snarled at the view-plate. "You absolutely won't get out of the disk if I land it?"

"No."

"Then die, you fool," said Mac, the words half-strangled in his throat; and he sent the ship rocketing through space like a meteor.

ALAN had felt Mac's mind leave his when Brave started to argue. He had concentrated furiously then on what he could do to overpower the alien. Very little of worth had occurred to him; but as a last resort he had determined on quick physical violence. If he could move as fast as Mac said he could, there was a chance.

Now, as the disk shot forward, he sensed Mac reaching out to touch his brain again, and with all his will he thought of other things, anything, anything except what he meant to do. He stared at the view-plate that showed the central roam. He could feel almost no sensation of motion, and Win seemed quite all right. But the three men were curled in their chairs, gasping, even the mighty Indian writhing under horrible, painful pressure.

"For the love of God, Mac!" cried Alan.

And McEldownie slowed the ship. He turned a sickened, saddened countenance to Alan. "I can't do it," he said a little pitifully. "I can't kill that big red devil. I like him too well. I think he knew that when he made his proposition. I don't care how much it delays me, I've got to land him. Hear that, Lo?" he said to the viewer. "I'm going to do it. I'll put your whole precious gang out on land, and find some of my own boys. Project Star will be the place, if I can get there without interference. I can load up my crew and a few of the painless gentry and it'll make a better army than this would have been.

But dammit, I did want my protege Alan with me."

"Say your dog, rather," suggested Alan bitterly.

"All right. Didn't you ever love a dog?"

"Yes."

"It's the same with me. I can't help feeling your race is inferior, but I can still be good and sorry to see you die, I can still feel affection for you."

"And that makes up for what you have been doing to him and the others?" asked Bill weakly.

"Oh, hell!" Mac bit his lip. "You are an impossible breed, you Earthlings."

Alan felt his mind withdraw again as he angled the disk around toward the west. In that instant, shoving aside the already unbuckled strap from his chest, and drawing the long hunting knife from its sheath at his side, he pounced out of his chair full upon the alien. Mac's green eyes flew open as Alan, his movements blurred by his incredible quickness caught the outlander's chin and dragged it back and with the other hand pressed the edge of the keen knife against the brown throat. Then, as he collected his startled thoughts, Alan said briskly, "Don't do it, Mac. Don't even think about touching my brain, because it's clear as a bell right now, and the first feeling I have of your meddling with it, I'm going to drag this knife through your windpipe. You can't control me without at least half a second's preparation, and with the reflexes you've given me, that's enough." He glanced up at the viewer. "Brave, Rob, don't either of you try to tell me anything telepathically. I know the different sensations I get when I'm being paged or controlled, and the first whimper of one of them sends this blade into Mac's neck."

NO one spoke for a moment. Then Mac said, "If you knew how ridiculous you look, standing there with that whopping carver and with that sick cat on your shoulder, I really believe you'd give this business up and bust out laughing."

"Don't count on it," said Alan levelly. "I'll tell you what, Mac. You said you were going to let us all go. Maybe you were. But I don't trust you worth an inflated nickel. You'd have found a way to get Win and me back. Besides that, we only have your side of the story, and about a tenth of it, at that. I want to meet some of these birds that bombed our cities. They told Rob, before you had me murder them, that they had made a mistake. They had to kill someone but they didn't mean to kill us. That someone was obviously you. I want to know why. If I let you and this saucer get out of my hands, and then find that the bombers are in the right in whatever quarrel they have with you, I'll be sorry the rest of my life. So you're going to take us to them, Mac. We're going to get the whole story."

McEldownie laughed. It was a completely mirthless noise, "Kiwanawatiwa," he said to Brave, "I have you to thank for this mutiny, you and those hypnosis gimmicks of yours."

"No, not altogether," said Alan. The knife pressed in a little and the tall man winced. "It was your admission that you were my voice," *My beloved voice in the depths of space,* he thought, almost ruefully. *It was fearful but I loved it.* "If you hadn't wanted to brag, you might have kept control of me."

"I wasn't bragging. I wanted you as an ally and friend, rather than a puppet."

"Robot is the word. You used it a couple of times."

"Not for you, damn it. I liked you as a fellow human being."

Something flicked at Alan's mind with feathery tentacles: the knife drew blood and the feathery searching stopped. "That hurts," objected Mac.

"It'll hurt worse. Take us to the nearest disk you know

of."

"How would I know of any?"

"You can find them. Do it."

"Don't push me too far," said the other icily. "Remember I'm infinitely stronger than you."

"But very susceptible to a sliced up jugular."

"I won't wreck five hundred years of plans, even for you!"

"Not for me," said Alan easily. "For the sake of your throat, Mac old boy."

Mac sighed, and turned the ship gently, for fear of the deadly blade in Alan's remorseless hand, and sent it rocking over the hills inland.

"I'm a weak link," he said bitterly. "A weak link like poor old Grady. I didn't know I'd be so afraid to die."

CHAPTER TWELVE

THEY landed gently beside the two great silver disks, and Mac sat back and said, "Well," proudly, for it was his first landing in half a millennium. "Now what, Jack the Ripper?"

"Now we go out and talk to them. First we let the gang out of the middle room, though."

Mac flipped a switch. "They can open the door now."

Brave and the others came to meet them in the corridor. They all had their rifles at the ready. "Put up the knife, Alan," said Rob Pope. "He's under control pretty well, I'd say. One phony move or thought and he's done."

Mac looked at them all. "I liked you," he said sadly. "I suppose I'll have to kill you eventually, but I did like you." Then they marched him down the ramp to the ground.

Alan and Win and Rob were aware at once of the amazement that ran through the alien forces like a Chinook wind among pines. Alan could catch the thoughts plainly: *It is he, it is the leader!*

"Holy cats," he said, and Unquote stirred feebly but angrily on his shoulder. "Mac, are you the chief of your bunch?"

"Yes. Oh, laddie, I'm a prize catch. They'll give you the Iron Cross for me. Or the Lead Casket."

The outlanders, duplicates in form and clothing of the men slain by Alan and the others, clustered around them. Alan wondered if there was hatred in his brain to be found by these fellows. He did not actually know himself whether or not he hated them for their bombing. The destruction of New York had been such a gargantuan thing, such an incredibly huge blow, that the solution of smaller problems seemed to have driven it out of his thoughts entirely; perhaps it was a trick of his subconscious, to prevent his going mad with horror.

He could hear them—if "hear" was the verb—talking mentally together. There was no language involved, evidently, for the thoughts were surely as plain to him as to the aliens themselves. "It's like listening in on an old-fashioned party line," he told Win.

"Isn't it—I mean," she added hastily, "I'm not old enough to remember, but it must be."

Alan grinned. "As I catch it, they're congratulating each other on capturing Mac. And by glory, they're thanking us!"

"They just unfolded my mind like a road map," said Rob, "so they know about all that we know. What stupendous capacities for absorption their brains must have! I get the feeling that they just glance through a kind of card index that's in the back room of my skull, and then they know how I feel about them, and about chess and women, and what I had for supper last night."

"It's not that miraculous," said McEldownie, on whose

wrists two of the aliens in filigreed harness had placed brass manacles connected by a long chain. "They—and I—touch the centers of emotion, and judge from them what sort of person you are. Just now they read the records of how you got the disk, and how you captured me; and they tried to find out how you reacted to the bombing of New York, but your emotion there was too obscure."

"I obscured it myself. I was ashamed of it. Because," said Rob, wrinkling up his forehead, "although I'm shaken when I think of it, and feel so sorry that *sorry* is a mild word, still I can't find any hatred for your brothers here. I honestly think it was a mistake on their part; and it must have been based on evidence, so that evidence was falsified; and only you and your crew could have done that. Ergo, I don't hate them. I hate you, Mac."

"You're all wrong."

"I'll find out before I do anything about it."

HALF a dozen of the bare-chested blond fellows came to stand before them. Again, there was no evidence of weapons—but whereas the first group had been careless after finding no basic hatred in Rob and Bill, this contingent had carefully studied the intent and the mental content of each of them. Probably, thought Alan, it was because they had brought McEldownie, who had been instantly recognized.

"That's right," said Mac in answer to his thought. "That first bunch were strangers to me. See the tall bloke with the argent headband? That's my uncle, my mother's brother. Half of this lot knew me at home."

"Mac," said Win, "where *is* your home?"

"Erin Grady told you the truth. We come from the ninth planet of a sun unknown to you."

"And why did you come?"

"That's a long yarn—and my uncle says he has something

to tell you." Mac shut his mouth. Tall, bony, homely, dressed in ordinary American clothes, his beak of a nose and the half-lidded green eyes so familiar to them all, Alan and the others felt a pang at seeing him silent and crestfallen among the fantastically clad outlanders. He was one of them, but he was also McEldownie, the TV announcer, the fellow who made bad puns and got drunk and ate enormously and suffered with them when New York died. Even Rob Pope, surer than the rest that Mac was at the bottom of all the hell unleashed that day, scowled and gave him a sorry grin.

"Maybe I'm planting the thought in your minds," Mac said cynically. None of them had spoken.

"I'd know if you were, I think," said Rob. "No, it's natural. You were a good egg."

"And as good eggs go, I went bad." He shrugged. "I think now that I didn't need to let you capture me for them. I might have killed Alan on the spot by touching a single button. Damn you all," he said without emotion, "I either loved you too well, or I was sick of running and being a rebel."

"A rebel against what?" asked Bill Thihling.

"Stuffiness and authority. I've got to shut up." He hung his head. He looked very tired and rather older than he had before this hour.

Then the leader of the aliens spoke to them. The message came in the curious wordless manner, and each of them put words to it in his own mind. To Alan it came like this:

"We are profoundly shocked at our hasty action of this morning. We have done you incomparable injury where a little more investigation would have shown us you were not inimical, not working against us, not bad at all as men go. Our only excuse is that we were direly pressed for time.

"We investigated certain sections of your planet where activities showed us some of the rebels from our world were at work; they were building ships and weapons to return to us, to attack us. We found at these places, some cities and some isolated deserts, some small towns and some government projects, that our rebels had taken control of your people, making them invulnerable with a ray that is known to us, making them long-lived and incapable of pain and with quickened reflexes and swifter bodies than before. To investigate this we should have had weeks. We gave ourselves less than a day. For we knew that our ships would have been sighted and the rebels would be speeding their plans. So we found many robot humans, many scientists working with our exiled people, and we thought that in all these places there must be millions of potential foemen."

THE message was charged with emotion; it was impossible to believe that the man was lying. Indeed, thought Alan, there was no reason why he should lie. If he could wipe out New York with one small golden egg, he had no need to make allies of a few puny humans.

"Again, our sole excuse is the lack of time. We did find many places where only a portion of those checked were under rebel control. Those places we did not bomb, trusting that if we struck the large cities and the projects where disk manufacture was under way, we could mop up the others with ground fighting."

I wonder if Project Star is gone, thought Alan.

"I wonder," echoed Win aloud. Then they turned to each other, astounded. "Darling," she said after a second, "that's the one thing I like about this hardening, pain-removing process—now we can talk to each other without words!"

"Think what we can do with our mouths while we're talking," he grinned.

The leader went on. "I may interject here that we took over control of your artificial satellite some days ago. We did not kill the men therein, who were not enemies, but controlled them by simple hypnosis. They will of course be freed of this as soon as our job is done and a peace settled on between our worlds."

Brave looked up at the sky. Albertus, of course, could not be seen with the naked eye, but he said, "I know a couple of the lads that run that space station. Good boys. I had been afraid they were dead. I knew they wouldn't have let us be smeared like this if they'd been able to prevent it."

"Only one city we bombed that we had not personally checked on; that is the large one over there," and he gestured toward Manhattan. "We could not send our men on the ground into that place; the entranceways are too complex, the place is too big, it would have taken too long; and we could scarcely fly over and drop spies. After earnest consultation we decided to bomb it. Being the largest concentration of civilized people in your world, being so close to the major rebel project, we felt—we *knew*—that it was full of enemies. Our stupidly-certain assumption was wrong. We can never make reparation for that mistake, we cannot begin to make amends to you. Your only help will be the knowledge that we will live with the memory of that mistake the rest of our lives; and they are long, long lives.

"We are men of good will. We beg you to believe this. We have outlawed war and our planet lives at peace, prosperous peace. Now we have committed an intolerable crime against a brother race. We are hurt, in our way, as much as you have been hurt."

BRAVE had taken Alan's hand in his own and was squeezing it hard; the scientist thought suddenly that if he were not impervious to pain, his hand would be aching like fury. Brave said, "Son, I need help," quite simply and humbly.

"What is it, Brave?"

"Alan, these people are good. They look like barbarians, they ride in twenty-second century vehicles, and they plaster our greatest cities into the earth. But they're good. He isn't lying."

"What's the problem, Brave?"

"I hate them," the Indian said fiercely. "I'd like to have them all here," he let go Alan's hand and jabbed a great forefinger at his palm. "I'd smash them like lice. I don't want to feel that way. It's primitive. But strip me of the veneer I've lost these last hours, and I'm primitive to the core. I'm simple and single-minded. I hate people who do me harm. I won't go berserk and start in on these gentry, but by heaven, by the Great Spirit, I'd like to wipe them all out—slaughter them all! I want to sacrifice them to the ghosts of our dead cities."

Alan said slowly, "And you don't want to feel that way. Because they're good, you want to forgive them their mistake. Good Lord, Brave," he cried, "how can we ever forgive them? We can understand them, but none of us will ever truly forgive and forget. Do you think because you feel that way that you are reverting to savagery? Then we're every one of us on the face of the earth pure howling savages!"

Brave searched his face. He nodded, "I see...I see what you're saying. I thought it was perhaps...just me. I guess I thought you would be shooting them down if you felt that way too. Sorry, boss."

Alan smiled grimly.

Rob said, "If we only knew a little more of the basic story, hang it! They haven't mentioned where they came from, why they exiled Mac's boys or why they chased after them, anything about themselves except that they made a mistake. We already know all that."

The leader put in urgently; "I sense many questions that I

would happily answer if I had the time. But I have just received word that our forces are massing to attack the disk project to the east of that large city. I must therefore leave you until the job is done."

"They're attacking Project Star!" said Win sharply. "Good Lord, Alan, we've got a hundred friends there!"

"Yes, and just as innocent people as those who died in Manhattan. They can't do it." He stepped forward—it was significant that not one alien tried to stop him—and laid a hand on the leader's bare, brawny arm. The flesh was almost normal...but not quite. Alan recalled Brave's suggestion of the feel of a rubber product. The arm was hairless and without pores, cool to the touch. He looked up into the leader's face. It was a good face, though the widened features gave it a somewhat aboriginal cast. It was a patriarchal face, more that of the ruler of a tribe than of the leader of a fleet of space disks who must also be an advanced scientist. The long yellow hair was turning slightly gray over the temples.

The man smiled. Yes, he said to Alan without words, I am over nine hundred years old.

"He comes from Shangri-La," said Bill Thihling. "He's the High Lama. You can't kid me."

Among his captors, the manacled McEldownie threw back his head and laughed. "That's what we needed," he said, "a good feeble jest. This meeting was getting dull as hell."

Alan ignored them. He tried to pierce into the leader's brain with his eyes, he thought fiercely and as hard as he ever had.

After three minutes the leader nodded. Alan turned to Brave. "Boy, we're going with them. We're going to lead the attack on Project Star."

"If you've got something up your sleeve—" began Rob.

"Nothing he doesn't know of. You think I'm able to keep my thoughts to myself? But we can save, or try to save, a lot of our people. Win stays here, of course. So does Rob, who has a bad leg." The leader gestured to another outlander who opened one of the numerous cases on the ground and took out bandages and salves in tins, with which he began to repair the burn on Pope's leg. "Bill," said Alan, "you want to come?"

"Try and dissuade me!"

"Cheers, then, gal," said Alan lightly, and kissed Win. He turned and went into the great disk via the bubble's ramp. Brave and Bill followed him. The leader and five of the others went up, leaving half a dozen with McEldownie and Win and Rob. Then Alan reappeared, looking sheepish, came down and handed a weary cat to the girl. "I've been wearing her on my shoulder for so long she thought she was growing there." He patted Unquote (who raked up the energy to spit at him) and disappeared once more. The disk rose silently into the air.

ALAN learned now that the aliens had a spoken tongue; for they began to chatter to each other, the sentences brief, the words evidently long and complex. It sounded a little like Latin, a little like Greek; but no words were even faintly familiar.

"What's your plan, Alan?" asked Brave.

"Not a very complex one, I'm afraid. We're to be allowed to go in first, the disk will fly low to avoid being sighted, and will land behind the hill that overlooks our house. We're to gain entrance naturally, if possible, or sneak in if the place is too heavily fortified and suspicious. I think we can walk right in. I'm patently a 'robot' and you two can be under my charge. Then we have an hour to contact everyone we can. We tell the fellows who are okay to collect in the chem lab. We try to persuade the robots to congregate in the welding room, where they can be captured easily and without bloodshed. But if we can't tell the difference between robots and aliens, then we pass along quick. We have to step high and fast, lads. And we can't separate to do the job, since you two can't check over the thoughts of the people we meet."

He stood up. "I'm going to wander around and get to know the boys. We'll be fighting on their side soon."

"I hope it's the right side."

"I think it is."

He walked over to the nearest group of aliens, who greeted him courteously. He found that when they spoke aloud he could not read their thoughts; but when they sensed that he believed them to be talking about him or about secrets they had from him, they at once went mute and directed their thought conversation to his brain cells. He sat down and began to ask questions. He found that he was able to do so now without strain.

"Yes," one of them told him, "your powers develop rapidly after the third exposure to the rays. Yet, they seem to come so gradually that you are hardly aware of them. It's a 'rapid gradualness,' so to speak."

Alan recalled that it was in the captured disk that he first felt the tremendous awakened power of his mind to read and feel the reciprocation of other minds. He nodded. They went on talking.

AT three-thirty p.m. of the day New York died, the three men walked up to the gate of Project Star. They carried their heavy rifles openly, and looked belligerent. It would have been hard to appear otherwise.

They were challenged by a soldier, who fronted a squad of men with flamers and grenade pistols. Before Alan could answer, the soldier said, "Oh, it's Dr. Rackham. Pass in, sir. Where'd you come from?"

"Manhattan."

"Cripes! you're lucky to be here." It was the same soldier who had passed him on the night of his treatment in the shed. He went into the colony, Brave and Bill Thihling at his heels.

At four-twenty-eight p.m. the three of them walked up close to the same gate. There were nine soldiers on duty. Beyond the fence were the ack-ack guns, radar detectors, and force field generators, manned by a number of other soldiers.

The three put their rifles down on the ground. Then they solemnly began to dance around in a little circle, unbuttoning their coats as they did so. The squad stared, moved uneasily a little closer, looked at their leader for guidance. He shrugged. He was a robotized fellow who had been made a particular pet by one of the aliens; he knew a great deal about the scheme of things in the colony—consciously, rather than unconsciously as most of them did—and was trusted above most of his fellows. He was not especially bright.

"They ain't breaking any rules," he said. "You never know what the hell a scientist is gonna do."

Brave and Alan and Bill had now divested themselves of their shirts. and were taking off their undershirts. They were still dancing their lilting small cakewalk.

"Nuts," said the soldier. "They're *nuts*. Musta caught some radiation from that mushroom buster." All the men on the ring of huge equipment beyond the fence were watching them too. It was amusing to see a really mad scientist and three that were overly delightful. They whooped and cheered and laughed.

Then the saucermen came over the hill.

It was as though they erupted from the ground, even to Alan and his henchmen who had been watching for them. And what a sight it was—barbarians in every physical trait, from face to naked chest to ornate girdle and gold loincloth, armed with tiny tubes that hurled fireballs and with thin blowpipes that shot numbing darts over incredible distances, they might have been warriors from a forgotten land in a long-forgotten time. And they came silently, so that they seemed to approach through the noiseless depths of a dream. But the shriek of a soldier falling from a gun platform, his face in flames. was not out of a dream, but a hideous nightmare.

THE three men pounced on their rifles, threw them up and were firing methodically even before they had regained the erect position. Alan and Brave, crack shots who had been used to practice every Sunday morning on the military range, shot for the heads; Bill, a less certain marksman, tried for the chests. The brain and heart were the only sure targets when you fought a man who could feel no pain and could keep going with half of his body shot away.

For a brief time it seemed to the soldiers that the scientists were shooting aliens; then the leader turned and saw where the muzzles pointed.

"Get 'em!" he bellowed, and sprayed a charge from a grenade pistol that went wide of its mark but fanned Bill's cheek with tiny scraps of hot breeze. Next instant he was down kicking from Bill's slug, and the guards of the gate were finished.

The vanguard of the outlanders swept in and across the grounds. They had concentrated on this single gate, as the approaches of the other gates were much too open for safety. There were men from sixteen saucers, over four hundred of them, and they ran like deer, like cheetahs after deer, like winds after cheetahs. Mutely, with a kind of ferocious impersonality, they descended on the colony.

Men came running out with machine guns and feverishly began to load them. They were picked off by rifle bullets, by paralyzing ray tubes, and relays came and were picked off and more came. One gun stuttered into action momentarily, and the crew went twisting up in the air, their gun blown apart, their bodies rent by a weapon that even Alan had not known of. He spotted it finally, a blunderbuss-shaped thing of silver with a flaring mouth, fired like a bazooka. Another machine gun blew up.

Among the buildings there was hand-to-hand combat, automatics against fire tubes, outlander against rebel outlander in wrestling, heaving confusion. All the men from the strange planet fought without speaking; the robots shouted, like normal men in a battle. Brave was bawling war whoops and Alan was cursing steadily, as he always did under fire. Bill Thihling had got himself lost somewhere.

The leader of Alan's saucer went by, blond hair streaming, blood dripping down the brown chest. Alan caught a thought:

Thanks.

He knew, from touching Alan's mind in passing, that many of the non-robot men and women were gathered in safety, and even a number of the alien-controlled puppets had been herded into the welding room and locked in, obedient to Alan's hypnotic order.

THE Indian and Alan came at last to the end of the ammunition that had bulged out their trouser pockets. They clubbed their rifles and waded into a melee that staggered back and forth between two office buildings, across the scarlet-stained grass. Then Alan lost his rifle, and drew his automatic. The range was always short and his hand was steady as a granite statue's. He was recognizing his foemen at every turn, and putting away the recognition and thinking, *They are rebels from the stars, mutineers against a good people, it was their plottings that brought on the smashing of our cities. This is not Dr. Coulterre, it's a creature eight hundred years old who wanted to make me into a brainless slave. That isn't Dr. Simms curled up with my bullet in his belly, it's the slayer of a million New Yorkers as sure as if it had put its own damned finger on the trip release.*

He could tell who the robots were because they yelled, and those he left alone, because the saucermen were shooting them with numbing rays that did not kill. It was a humane method as far as it went. Sometimes he had to blow a robot's brains out, or be slain by him. Then he said, I've killed a friend. He went looking for more aliens to fight.

In all the press of bodies Alan and Brave were easiest to see. Brave was huge and his head was that of a savage buck, the lips writhed back from teeth athirst for blood. Alan, naked to the waist and with a white bandage over his right ear, put on by a surgeon in the saucer, was a figure differing radically from the barbaric saucermen and the sedately-clothed rebels and robots. They had taken off their shirts in the dance for a better reason than holding the attention of the soldiers. Among a hundred men like them they would have been indistinguishable had they stayed fully clothed. It's simple, he thought to tell the good guys from the bad guys; the good guys haven't got any shirts.

The two of them made excellent targets. Brave knew he carried a slug in his leg just next the groin; Alan had no idea whether he had been hit. Enemies were continually firing at them both.

Alan was knocked to the turf by a man who leaped on his back and started beating at his head with a pistol butt. Brave swung the rifle, a truly terrible war club in his hands, and broke the man's head like a rotten gourd. Alan got up with the feeling that he should have a headache. But he felt nothing.

Then the rebel outlanders gave up. Suddenly, all over the scattered fields of battle, they had thrown down their weapons and thrust up their hands above their heads in the universal signal of surrender. Their robot people followed suit. The saucermen had won. Project Star was theirs.

CHAPTER THIRTEEN

THEY were back at the temporary base of the disks, sitting on the grass in the shade of the great ships, the sun just going down behind them. Brave's slug had been extracted and the wound bandaged with ointments that eased the pain. Bill Thihling, who had been knocked cold early in the fight, was sucking on a lozenge that was lessening his headache by the minute. Alan had not been shot and the beating his head had taken did not worry him, for pain was forever a stranger. He sat with Unquote asleep in his lap and Win's hand held tight in his.

"I don't want to live four hundred years," he said. "I want to die in the same years that Brave and my friends go. I don't want to be invulnerable; I want to stick myself with a needle and yell Ouch. I don't want to move like a hopped-up panther, and know what people are thinking, and send brainstorms out to sea from my little skull. I want to be me again." His words were light and half-whimsical, but his thoughts were black.

"Same here, darling," said the girl. She put up a hand to adjust her amethyst halter and his eyes followed it; she laughed. "At least your baser instincts are still intact, thank heavens."

Rob Pope said, "There's a helluva lot they still have to explain to us. We seem to have heard the final chapter of a thousand-page book. They haven't even said who they are, or which system they come from, or what Mac's gang did that they were exiled for."

"And by the way," said Win indignantly, "no one's told me

yet why they attacked Project Star on the ground instead of bombing it. Tell me..."

"Yes, love. They attacked it that way because they didn't want to damage any of the experimental stuff and the disks. They lost four disks in space, coming here, and they're overcrowded, besides having Mac's crew to take home for trial. They need disks. And they're interested in seeing what advances we may have made on fuel and instruments, advances that might give them ideas. All quite logical."

"Sure, sure. Everybody knew but Winnie."

"Between their numbing rays and our preliminary work, we managed to save nearly all the normal humans on the colony grounds, and about seventy per cent of the robots. There are aliens there now, guarding them and the disks and the whole project."

The leader came over to them and squatted on the grass, radiating intelligence and power. "There's quite a unique man," said Rob in spite of himself.

"I suppose he is at that. I wonder how such advanced people happened to evolve with such barbaric ornaments and clothing?" Win said.

THE leader smiled. Evidently the blood Alan had seen on his chest had been someone else's, for he was unhurt. Now he said to their minds, "The girdles and arm bands are traditional. They go back farther than the oldest histories, and date perhaps from our original home, which was on a different planet from our present one. We consider them attractive, if gaudy and a little unfitted for our sort of civilization. However, it would be unthinkable to change our mode of dress after so many centuries."

"And *that* is the attitude I rebelled against," said Mac aloud, from his place between two guards. "That's how they look at everything. Hell...can you blame me?" He stared at his manacled wrists. "I used to go around the cities in a kind of toga that appealed to my esthetic sense. Heavens…I was shunned. I was a pariah. No armband."

The leader smiled again. "My nephew exaggerates. Five hundred years haven't calmed that roiling renegade blood.

"I know what you are desirous of knowing. I will try to tell you the story simply and quickly, for I must join my companion ship within two hours in the island that I see you call England." He glanced at Brave and Alan. "First I must thank you for your indispensable help in overcoming the rebels at Project Star."

"We didn't do much for you."

"You fought beside us when you hated us for the bombing of your cities; that implies understanding, if not forgiveness. We appreciate that. You saved innocent lives; that is the best way to help us. To kill is a terrible thing to us. We do not do it lightly. To kill innocents, even in cases of dire necessity, is trebly terrible."

"Your men went at it as if they were born to it," said Brave.

"They do not like it, no, but there is a heritage in our blood of fighting that dates back, as do our clothes, to the times before history."

"Pious old fraud," said McEldownie, "you love it, but you won't admit it to yourselves. It was we rebels who were the honest ones."

The leader ignored him. "I was about to tell you—"

Mac said aloud, so that the leader's thought waves were garbled, "I could hate you two for running amok alongside these sniveling so-and-sos. You helped kill scores of my companions. You couldn't have been that sure we were wrong, could you? Damn it, I loved those boys. I lived with them for a dozen of your match-spark lifetimes."

"If you speak out of turn again, I shall have you taken into the leaded room of my disk, where your thoughts and words will be confined to yourself. I was about to tell you of our history," the leader thought, looking at Alan's group. "Long, long ago, so long that even we, who live a thousand years, cannot comprehend what a vast reach of time it was, we lived on a planet very like your own. The atmosphere must have been exactly, or nearly exactly, like that of Earth; for you and I have the same lungs, the same organs, and only differ fundamentally in the texture of our skins and the flexibility of our skeletons and muscles.

"Then, for a reason we do not know except by vague and undependable myth, our ancestors left that planet and went out into space. They were already superbly advanced scientists, though they did not have the rays later developed, which gave us our extended life span. They built disks and journeyed out into the star systems, and eventually found a planet that could support their life in the way the mother planet had done. There they settled. The old charts and logs and histories are long since lost, and this is known only by legend and tradition."

"What does legend say sent them away from the first planet?" asked Rob Pope.

"Several things. Terrible wars, the rise of inimical civilizations that would have had to be obliterated to insure peace, which our ancestors did not wish to do—"

"Bovine feces," muttered Mac rudely.

"—and the sinking of their homeland into the sea."

"Good grief," said Win, opening her eyes wide, "could that have been Atlantis? Here on Earth?"

"The time wouldn't seem to be right," said Bill, "but heaven only knows, it sounds like it."

The leader groped in their minds. "You have a legend of just such a nation here, on this planet," he thought excitedly. "We must investigate it. This may be our home." He chuckled aloud. "Don't worry, we wouldn't come back and settle in with you. We are too happy on our own world. But it would be wonderfully satisfying to know the truth of our beginnings."

ALAN felt himself becoming intellectually agog over this matter, and resolutely drew away from it. "Please," he said, "your history…"

"Certainly. On the new planet, which we call Tlonis, our race set up a civilization that has endured for many millenia. Our ancestors found no intelligent race on that world, by the way, but only low forms of animal life. The flora is analogous to your own in many ways, as is natural when two planets are so alike.

"For all our recorded history we have been a peaceful people, although in the course of our scientific advancement we have discovered terrible weapons, which we manufactured and put aside in the always possible case of invasion from another system. Our own sun system, in which Tlonis is the ninth planet from the sun, contains no other life at all; but we recognized the possibilities, and built the weapons to be ready. We also improved the disks, and discovered the ray of longevity and that of painlessness. Our astronomy was always our first science, and there I venture to say we outshine you as your sun does your moon."

"He's right," said Mac suddenly, looking up. "Tlonis telescopes make your giant eye of Mt. Palomar look like a gnat's. If you had one here, you could see a candle lighted on the sun."

"Your turn is coming—be silent. We have always existed in excellent harmony with one another. Wars are unknown. There is no such thing as territorial expansion, for we are all one nation, one blood. The government is a form of benevolent parliamentary rule."

McEldownie did not venture to interrupt, but his homely face spoke bookshelves of disdain.

"Our joys were intellectual, a reveling in rationality, philosophy and perception of truths, metaphysical reasoning. I am speaking in the past tense; I should not be. These are the things which have always occupied us, and always will."

"Sounds deadly dull," said Rob Pope, and Mac grinned and shook his head in vigorous agreement.

The leader then went on. "This sounds too placid to you. We are a different race, remember. It fits our temperaments perfectly.

"But there are members of any society whose tastes run counter to the norm of that society. In our case, in our time, it was this nephew of mine and his faction who rebelled. First in dress, as he has said, then by initiating the custom of hunting and killing the lower forms of life for sport, a thing unheard of before they originated it. This was their first serious breach of our laws and customs. From it they went on—talking against the government, decrying traditions, until at last their mania to be different intensified and turned to violence. In short, they mutinied against the established order of things that had made our race a happy one for untold ages. They wished to substitute ways of life that would have torn us apart with dissension and strife."

"We rebelled against complacency, fat-headedness, hidebound slavishness to tradition, and unutterable dullwitted dullness. You can appreciate that, for cripe's sake," said Mac. "Picture the way of life he's given you a briefing on, and tell me that you, especially Alan and Brave, wouldn't have rebelled—even if it meant war—to be allowed the right to live your own lives."

Alan and the great Indian looked at each other. The same thought was in both their minds—it sounded as though Mac and his outlaw crew had been in the right.

THE leader directed a thought at them. "You must realize that this man, my nephew, was not content to share his views with those who agreed with him. He forced an insurrection on a people who had been thoroughly happy. There was bloodshed in a race that had known none for generations. We overcame him and we might have executed him, but it was repugnant to us. So we gave him space disks and fuel and synthetic food machines and all else he would need, he and the men who had fought for him, and we exiled him to space.

"We knew that somewhere there was a planet that could sustain life. He had a chance of finding it, a small chance, but a chance nevertheless. As it happens, he *did* find it."

"After three hundred years of the blackness of the void," said McEldownie. "It was the mercy of God that we did. Otherwise we'd have lived out our lives in space. Do you see the cruelty that lurks in these people, which they won't recognize? Killing us would have been kind; but they sent us to wander among the galaxies."

"You may tell them briefly what you did then," the leader ordered him. "Be quick, my time is nearly up."

Mac stood up and walked back and forth, clinking his chained manacles. "We found Earth because our detectors told us the atmosphere was the same as that of our world. It was the only one of its kind we'd come across in all those centuries, centuries of sweeping through sun system after sun system.

"Maybe it's the original home planet our ancestors left, and maybe it isn't. I've mucked around with that Atlantis theory too. The names are similar—Atlantis, Tlonis. It isn't important.

"We landed in the late years of your eighteenth century. Our disks were seen and you can still find records of the sightings in the books and periodicals of that time, and of later times when our lads took the ships out of hiding for practice flights. I never practiced because it's only in the last forty years my crippling wounds have been really healed.

"We more or less took you over. It was reprehensible from your point of view. Don't hate me for it. We had to make you advance a thousand years' worth in two hundred. We wanted to go back to Tlonis and—not conquer it, but make a place for our kind of thinking so we could live there. It's home, after all. We needed disks and an army.

"Sure, we kept you in a stew, worked up, always at war, and so on. It was the only way. You'd always warred before, anyway. Only in times of war could we advance your knowledge of science and make its rapidity seem logical. So we controlled governments and laboratories and brains. If we hadn't, you'd still be in the gunpowder stage, instead of the jet and electronic stage. We aren't all bad. We aren't pure black. We hurt you as little as we could. We used you in the same way that you used to use oxen and horses. But just like you, we loved horses…which often got killed in war mind you…but still, we loved you."

"Stop apologizing, Mac. We understand your point of view," said Alan. "But we understand this man's, too."

"Sure, sure. Everybody has a right to his own opinion, even if it's a stuffy one.

"Anyhow, in the early '40s we gave you the atom bomb, nuclear fission, that is. And the radiations of those first bombs went out across the great spaces, and twelve years later were detected and analyzed on Tlonis by the astronomers. Uncle's bunch got in an uproar, as we'd known they would, and piled into ships and started out for Earth. We couldn't help that. We'd had to give you fission. We figured we had enough time. We started disk construction and we began to build an invincible army out of your men, by dousing them with the painkilling and telepathic rays. We miscalculated the time it would take Uncle to get here. We wanted to meet him in space or bypass him and get to Tlonis with our followers. Maybe, we thought, he wouldn't have connected the atomic explosion with us—but he did, and he knew we were preparing to invade Tlonis...so he came.

"His scouting ships reached Earth a few months ago, reported back to the main fleet, and down he came, to blunder and take things for granted and make too-hasty decisions, as always; and he murdered more people through hastiness than we ever would have in our scheme of things."

THE leader thought bitterly, "I admit the truth of that. I have said we are more sorry than we can ever tell." He gestured at Alan. "Consider this as you weigh what my nephew has said. There is a false sense of kinship between you because of the mutual language. He talks while I must telepath my thoughts to you. Discount that when you judge us, please."

Mac said, "That's right. When you sit down to think us over, just consider the stories, not who told them. I believe you'll agree with my way of thinking, whether you hate me for what I've done or not." He moved over in front of Brave. "Oh, you great iron-faced ruffian, you lost me my world, I think. Simply because I liked you too well to kill you, you and your sidekick here. Believe that or not. I have a real affection for you."

It seemed important to the lanky alien. Brave said, "I believe you, Jim."

"Thanks, Brave." He grinned. "Will you shake hands with a fallen angel, or if you prefer with an ambitious devil, John Kiwanawatiwa?"

Brave stood and took his hand. Alan and Bill, Rob and Win did likewise. There was something paradoxically touching about the little ceremony. Then the leader thought at them, "We will take him back for trial, him and those of his mutineers who are still alive. There are some still free in your world. With your permission we will stay on Earth until we have hunted them down. We would also like to study your histories, out of intellectual curiosity, and exchange scientific knowledge with you. These things can be arranged with your governments after their members have been freed from the hypnosis applied by our rebels."

He paused. "But we owe you this. You are representative of the people of this world. I give you the right to speak for all of them now. Shall we leave you? You hate us, will always hate us for what we did out of blindness and hasty folly. If you say so, you five, then we will get into our ships and go home."

Alan was a little staggered. "We can't speak for our country."

"I am not interested in governments, which are in reality artificial things. I am interested in the people of this planet, and I think you five can speak for them."

Alan did not hesitate. "Then I say, stay until you've found the rebels, and until you've made your researches. You're right...I believe we'll hate you. But it would be insane to pack you off and lose all that you can give us, or have you lose what we may be able to teach you."

The leader smiled. "Then we will stay." He turned to his men and gave an order; shortly many of the blond aliens came trooping out of the disk, carrying machinery. They proceeded to set it up before the Earthmen.

The leader told them, "These will be used on all of you who were tricked or cajoled or forced into the beams of the mutation rays by my nephew and his cohorts. Please stand quietly."

Shafts of violet and indigo color shot out of the lenses of

the machines. It took a full ship's complement of men to work all of them. The lights played across Alan and Win, to a lesser degree on Brave and the scientists. There was no sensation from them.

Then Alan said, "Wow! That hurts my ear something fierce."

Win turned to him. "Your ear hurts, darling?"

"Like a red hot iron."

Brave clamped his hands on his friend's biceps. "Emir! You can feel pain!"

"Pain…my Lord, blessed pain! Damn how it burns! I've got a splitting headache, too." Alan hit Brave in the chest, laughing, and then embraced Win. "Baby, I can feel pain! I'm okay—" He kissed her savagely. She gave a shriek.

"You bit me, you—Alan, I can feel it too!"

"Of course," the leader told them. "You are whole again. The effect of my nephew's rays is dissipated."

Alan sobered. "One thing. Will I still live four hundred years?"

"No. That effect is gone too, unfortunately."

Alan stared around him at his friends. "Thank God," he said quietly.

Then Rob Pope said, "Look, the bubble of that disk is closing!"

IT was true. The leader of the outlanders turned and saw it and gave a loud cry. "He's escaping! You let him out of your sight, you fools!" he thought angrily. All the gold-and-silver-clad men ran toward the disk. It rose into the air, flipping its edges impudently. Then it gathered speed and shot out of sight.

Brave said, "Jim, old Jim! He's made his break. I kind of thought he would. He was too restless a spirit to sit calmly under chains and captivity."

The aliens had clustered together and were sending their brain waves out across the land, signaling other disks in remote spots to find and pursue the escaping McEldownie. Alan said, "I almost hope he makes it..."

Then straight across the sky from horizon to horizon a great silver ship flashed, bright in the rays of the vanished sun against a darkening violet-blue sky, on its way out to sea in the direction of Africa. The abandoned outlanders were piling into their second disk to give chase.

Brave put his arm over Alan's shoulders. "Chief, I hope he makes it too. Maybe he was Lucifer, fallen and using us as dogs of war to regain his lost kingdom, or maybe he was really Prometheus, fighting the stodgy gods to bring fire—the fire of real freedom—to his friends. By his lights, he was justified in using us to do it. He caused us an awful throng of troubles in the past two hundred years, but what he gave us may be worth it in the final estimate. And when he had his goal in sight he threw it away because he couldn't bring himself to kill us."

"Prometheus is the word, son. I'd hate to see old Zeus there bring him back in chains, to be bound to the rock for the vultures."

Brave looked into the sky where Jim McEldownie had disappeared. He chuckled deep in his chest.

"He claimed to be the best hotshot disk pilot in the universe. If he is, I have a notion he'll get away." He rubbed a hand across his chin reflectively. "By the Great Spirit!" he shouted, laughing. "I believe he will!"

THE END

If you've enjoyed this book, you will not want to miss these terrific titles…

ARMCHAIR SCI-FI, FANTASY, & HORROR DOUBLE NOVELS, $12.95 each

D-1 **THE GALAXY RAIDERS** by William P. McGivern
SPACE STATION #1 by Frank Belknap Long

D-2 **THE PROGRAMMED PEOPLE** by Jack Sharkey
SLAVES OF THE CRYSTAL BRAIN by William Carter Sawtelle

D-3 **YOU'RE ALL ALONE** by Fritz Leiber
THE LIQUID MAN by Bernard C. Gilford

D-4 **CITADEL OF THE STAR LORDS** by Edmund Hamilton
VOYAGE TO ETERNITY by Milton Lesser

D-5 **IRON MEN OF VENUS** by Don Wilcox
THE MAN WITH ABSOLUTE MOTION by Noel Loomis

D-6 **WHO SOWS THE WIND…** by Rog Phillips
THE PUZZLE PLANET by Robert A. W. Lowndes

D-7 **PLANET OF DREAD** by Murray Leinster
TWICE UPON A TIME by Charles L. Fontenay

D-8 **THE TERROR OUT OF SPACE** by Dwight V. Swain
QUEST OF THE GOLDEN APE by Ivar Jorgensen and Adam Chase

D-9 **SECRET OF MARRACOTT DEEP** by Henry Slesar
PAWN OF THE BLACK FLEET by Mark Clifton.

D-10 **BEYOND THE RINGS OF SATURN** by Robert Moore Williams
A MAN OBSESSED by Alan E. Nourse

ARMCHAIR SCIENCE FICTION CLASSICS, $12.95 each

C-1 **THE GREEN MAN**
by Harold M. Sherman

C-2 **A TRACE OF MEMORY**
By Keith Laumer

ARMCHAIR MASTERS OF SCIENCE FICTION SERIES, $16.95 each

M-1 **MASTERS OF SCIENCE FICTION, Vol. One**
Bryce Walton—"Dark of the Moon" and other tales

M-2 **MASTERS OF SCIENCE FICTION, Vol. Two**
Jerome Bixby: "One Way Street" and other tales

If you've enjoyed this book, you will not want to miss these terrific titles...

ARMCHAIR SCI-FI & HORROR DOUBLE NOVELS, $12.95 each

D-11   **PERIL OF THE STARMEN** by Kris Neville
THE STRANGE INVASION by Murray Leinster

D-12   **THE STAR LORD** by Boyd Ellanby
CAPTIVES OF THE FLAME by Samuel R. Delaney

D-13   **MEN OF THE MORNING STAR** by Edmund Hamilton
PLANET FOR PLUNDER by Hal Clement and Sam Merwin, Jr.

D-14   **ICE CITY OF THE GORGON** by Chester S. Geier and Richard S. Shaver
WHEN THE WORLD TOTTERED by Lester Del Rey

D-15   **WORLDS WITHOUT END** by Clifford D. Simak
THE LAVENDER VINE OF DEATH by Don Wilcox

D-16   **SHADOW ON THE MOON** by Joe Gibson
ARMAGEDDON EARTH by Geoff St. Reynard

D-17   **THE GIRL WHO LOVED DEATH** by Paul W. Fairman
SLAVE PLANET by Laurence M. Janifer

D-18   **SECOND CHANCE** by J. F. Bone
MISSION TO A DISTANT STAR by Frank Belknap Long

D-19   **THE SYNDIC** by C. M. Kornbluth
FLIGHT TO FOREVER by Poul Anderson

D-20   **SOMEWHERE I'LL FIND YOU** by Milton Lesser
THE TIME ARMADA by Fox B. Holden

ARMCHAIR SCIENCE FICTION CLASSICS, $12.95 each

C-3   **INTO PLUTONIAN DEPTHS**
by Stanton A. Coblentz

C-4   **CORPUS EARTHLING**
by Louis Charbonneau

C-5   **THE TIME DISSOLVER**
by Jerry Sohl

C-6   **WEST OF THE SUN**
by Edgar Pangborn

ARMCHAIR SCIENCE FICTION & HORROR GEMS SERIES, $12.95 each

G-1   **SCIENCE FICTION GEMS, Vol. One**
Isaac Asimov and others

G-2   **HORROR GEMS, Vol. One**
Carl Jacobi and others

www.ingramcontent.com/pod-product-compliance
Lightning Source LLC
Chambersburg PA
CBHW030310180626
46810CB00003B/1008